Bloody Kisses
A Vampire Erotica Anthology

Dark Moon Press

Bloody Kisses

A Vampire Erotica Anthology

Dark Moon Press

Cover art by

Warlock Corvis Nocturnum

Cover Design and Layout by

Dark Moon Press

Published by

Dark Moon Press

Copyright 2007 Dark Moon Press

ISBN# 978-0-6151-6783-1

Bloody Kisses

A Vampire Erotica Anthology

is published by Dark Moon Press

Ft. Wayne, Indiana

For a full catalogue of Dark Moon's publications refer to

http://www.darkmoonpress.net

Or send an SASE to:

P.O. Box 11496, Ft. Wayne, Indiana, 46858-1496

Or send an SASE to:

Dark Moon Press

P.O. Box 11496, Fort Wayne, Indiana 46858-1496

TABLE OF CONTENTS

Consuming Desire

Michelle Belanger

The room was done in burgundy and gold, with woodwork of a rich mahogany. The gaslights were dim, the air was moist and warm, and the overall effect was one of stepping into some internal chamber of a living body. A sturdy four-poster bed dominated one half of the room. The dark wood of the bedframe was attractively carved, and each leg ended in a large, clawed foot. Amidst the ornate carving, the metal eyelets were innocuous, almost invisible. Hiding beneath a decorative ruffle on the base of the bed were thick leather straps that were undoubtedly constructed to encircle the entire width of the mattress, accommodating a body within their clasp as well.

A mirror ran the length of the wall opposite the bed. Several feet away from the mirrored walled, various chains hung from fixtures in the ceiling. Additional eyelets in the ceiling seemed to be arranged for the attachment of a swing. A large chest rested up against the foot of the bed. A similar chest lay up against the wall between the pole and the footrest. Above it, various switches, rods, crops, and floggers hung from a wooden rack. A door opposite us stood partly open, revealing the water closet beyond.

"Perfect," I smiled, my hunger surging. The sense of consummations past clung to the place.

Beside me, Elizabeth studied the various apparatus scattered throughout the room. If the bondage equipment made her uneasy, she made no outward sign. I placed an arm around her shoulder, guiding her through the door. Softly, I let it close behind us. It locked automatically.

"Will you take off your dress?" I asked. "Or shall I do that for you?"

"Help me," she said softly. "But only the dress. I want my corset to stay on. And my bloomers. For now."

I helped her undo the many little buttons that ran down the back of her dress. It was made of a lightweight material, probably cotton, and was a slightly darker blue than her gloves. It had a high collar that covered her up to her neck. It would have looked quite chaste, except for a lace panel that opened up over the bodice. This revealed her bust line while giving the impression of concealing it as well. I found the overall effect tantalizing.

I finished with the final button and slid her dress to the floor. Her corset was ivory in color and severely nipped at her waist. It started just under her breasts and ran down to her hips. Above the corset, her breasts were full and firm, the nipples a rich pink against her creamy skin. Her bloomers were simple white cotton, fringed with delicate lace.

I ran my hands down the length of her body, almost -- but not quite -- touching her flesh. She shivered in response. Suddenly modest, she sat back down on the edge of the bed and held her arms protectively up over her breasts. I settled down a few inches beside her.

"We've come this far," I said. "Will you give me a kiss?"

She turned her head to face me, but demurred.

"You have to give in just a little," I urged.

"I'm afraid," she breathed, then suddenly in a saucier tone, she said, "I can't give in. You shall have to take me."

She regarded me coyly from beneath her golden lashes. There was no fear in her expression, just that aching, brittle, yearning.

Gently, I ran one hand through her thick fall of golden hair. Before she could react, I twined my fingers at the base of her neck, pulling her head back so her eyes met mine.

"I hope you know what you're asking," I said, then bore her down upon the pillows of the bed.She thrashed against me, golden hair flying.

"No!" She gasped. "Wait! What are you going to do to me?"

Pinning her wrists, I asked, "What do you want me to do with you?"

She bit her lower lip.

"I don't know what I want!" she cried plaintively.

"That's what got us here in the first place, remember?" I asked. "Do you want this? I can take you places you've never dreamed of, Elizabeth. But you have to want it."

"I'm afraid of what I want," she moaned. "I'm afraid that I'll want it too much. I'll never get enough. I'll become consumed!"

I pressed the length of my body against hers, still gripping her wrists. I felt her shudder from head to toe. She closed her eyes against it, still fighting her desires.

"I know you want this," I told her, rubbing my cheek against hers. "You wouldn't come to a place like this, watching the patrons night after night if you didn't want it. I've seen you. I've tasted that aching, yearning desire. You wouldn't have come to these back rooms with me if you didn't want to surrender."

Beneath me, she whimpered, catching her lip between her teeth to keep it from trembling.

"I could tie you up," I offered. "Then you would have to submit to whatever I did to you."

I felt her tremble again.

"You'd like that, wouldn't you?" I chuckled. "Please, Elizabeth. I'm hungry for you."

She tossed her head madly against the pillows, fighting her desire as strongly as she yearned to give in to it.

Finally, she said, "I want to be consumed!"

Her eyes looked like they would shatter with the truth of it.

Smiling with carefully closed lips, I pressed my cheek against hers, breathing in the scent of her. She whimpered and squeezed her eyes shut. My mouth found hers, and her lips yielded to me. I started very slowly, kissing first her upper lip, then sucking on the lower one. Only after I had explored all that her lips had to offer did I press my tongue beyond them. She fought this briefly, then welcomed my more intimate exploration of her mouth. I ran my tongue over her teeth, caressing the insides of her lips, her cheeks, then filling her entire mouth with me. She struggled with her tongue, but then began to answer my thrusts with cautious little probings of her own. I leaned into her, wrapping my hands around her wrists, completely giving myself over to the sensation of her mouth. Her chest heaved against mine as she struggled for breath. I felt her walls begin to slip, and she started to become mine.

Once we had been kissing forever, and our two mouths were the only things we had ever known, I pulled away from her. She opened and shut her mouth after I withdrew, her lips searching for me. I was staring into her eyes when she finally opened them again. She returned my deep stare, loosing a tremulous susurration of breath.

"You ... " was all she said.

I kissed her lips again briefly, then began showering quick little kisses all over her face, her cheeks, her eyebrows, her forehead, the tails of her eyes. This was not what she expected, but she accepted this gentle onslaught, closing her eyes to focus more intensely on the physical sensations. I kissed the lids of her eyes, running my tongue over the delicate, salty-tasting skin there. I traced a delicate line of kisses from her jaw, down the pale line of her throat. At the base of her neck, where it curved into shoulder, I gathered the tender skin between my teeth and gently bit down, rolling her flesh against my tongue. She gasped at first, but this soon gave way to a moan. Her little hands were balled into tight little fists now, the knuckles whitening.

"Beautiful," I whispered to her, loosing her wrists. She kept her arms thrown back over her head where I had left them. Her submission was sublime.

She leaned into my caress as I traced the golden arch of one eyebrow with my finger. I ran my fingers down the curve of her cheek, lingered in the hollow of her jaw, then slid along her neck to her collar bone, brushing the lingering teeth marks with the backs of my nails. My touch was light as the kiss of a butterfly's wings. My fingertips tingled, and I flexed them momentarily. I focused everything that I was into my burning hands. I touched the warmth beyond her flesh, shaped it, drew it out. She sensed this, and shuddering, loosed a soft sound deep in her throat.

"What are you doing?" she began. "What is that?"

But I pressed my fingers to her lips, hushing her.

"Never mind what it is," I said. "Just enjoy it."

As I caressed her lightly all over, I reached my energy into her, seeking to touch something much deeper than skin. I felt the connection building between us, and I drew upon it gently. She moaned and trembled, straining beneath my weight, though all I had done was lay my hands against her body. I closed my eyes, focusing on a place past physical sight, striving to draw forth her pleasure, savoring the molten golden flame it began to evoke within her. I could feel little strands of my fire extend into her, running along her nerves and seeking the most delicate places from within. The resulting climaxes were slow and gentle, but relentless. They started at the very core of her, and I could practically watch them tremble all the way to her fingers.

"Oh, God," she cried. "Oh, God. What? How? Oh, God!"

It was a song of supplication, a song of praise. She glowed like a dying saint, tossing her head against the pillows until her hair was glorious tangle.

As she was lost in this unexpected orgasm, I slid off of her and bent to the chest at the foot of the bed. Inside were all manner of restraints. Thick manacles of leather seemed too severe for the delicate carnal flower I had stretched out upon the bed. I withdrew instead silken scarves of Tyrian hue.

Before returning to the bed, I removed my vest and shoes, then stripped off my shirt as well. She watched me longingly as I folded these and laid them over the nearby chair. Her eyes studied my hairless chest, the slim waist tapering to narrow hips, the wiry muscles that stood out beneath smooth, golden-tan skin.

"Do you like what you see?" I inquired, absently rubbing the silk of the scarves against my skin.

"You look like a statue," she responded. "Not like a man at all."

"I never claimed to be a man," I told her, leaning over her on the bed once more. "I am something far more interesting."

This evoked a strange expression from her, but I did not give her the chance to question things for long. I grabbed one slender wrist, wrapping the scarf around it and tying it to the bedpost.

"Now let us begin our exploration of you in earnest."

Once she was tied firmly to the bed and could no longer resist, I tore her out of the rest of her clothes, leaving only the elegant ivory corset. Once I had removed her bloomers, I tied her ankles as firmly to the bed as I had tied her wrists. She watched me through half-lidded eyes, already languorous with ecstasy. I caressed and bit her by turns, running my hands lightly along her flesh one moment, dragging sharp nails against her skin the next. She submitted to every new sensation, pleasure and pain commingled, each touch of flesh against flesh stoking her desire.

Although she was stretched naked before me, I left all of the forbidden areas untouched, using my gifts to reach through her, evoking her passion from the inside. The orgasms this inspired were protracted and sweet, and I used the same subtle fire to pull the pleasure from her to me, drinking in her passion. I was not ignorant of the growing heat between her thighs, or the way she thrashed to rub her legs together as she lay tied upon the bed.

"Do you want me?" I whispered, starting to unfasten my trousers.

Her eyes closed tight against the waves of pleasure, she nodded.

"Say it," I urged.

She gasped as even then I ran my hands along her flesh, sending cascades of sensation up and down her limbs.

"Yes!"

I smiled, careful to keep my lips closed, for now I could feel the eyeteeth pressing against the inside of my mouth. She looked up as I knelt over her, removing my belt and sliding out of my pants. Her eyes strayed to the long, slender column of flesh nested in a patch of reddish blond hair.

"I want you," I said carefully. I leaned over her, letting the weight of me press against her mound. "Will you give yourself to me?"

"Yes! Please, yes!" she cried, raising her hips beneath me and thrashing.

This time I allowed myself to smile. Her eyes flew wide, but their look was one of hunger, not of fear.

"Thank you."

The heat of her practically scalded me as I pressed in. At the same moment that I pushed into her, I bent once more to that stretch of flesh at the base of her neck. This time, I bit in earnest, scraping my teeth against her sweet flesh just hard enough to open two shallow cuts. As the hot salt of her flooded my mouth, I pounded into her, feeling heat and wet within and without. I twined the fingers of one hand into her tangled, golden tresses, cupping my other hand around her breast, teasing the nipple with my thumb. There was nowhere inside of her that I did not touch with my energy, and her nerves were a harp of tender flesh that I plied with every aspect of my being.

Our two bodies fell into a desperate rhythm, my mouth locked tight upon her lest I lose even the smallest drop of precious life. Every thrust evoked a gasp from her, and the sounds escalated into wordless, ecstatic cries. The culmination we shared together left us both limp and spent, tangled limb to limb upon the bed.

When I could move again, I dragged my tongue across the shallow wound at the base of her neck, catching the last precious drops. Her heart was pounding so wildly, I could feel its vibrations against my cheek even though I was not actually touching her. Gradually, I drew away. She lay, spent and languid in her bonds. I placed my head upon her belly, cradling her for a while. Then, before she began to stir, I began untying her. At first, her limbs were limp in my hands. Her eyes were partly closed, and she hovered somewhere between sleep and unconsciousness. I rubbed circulation back into her fingers, then folded her hands over her belly. The folds of the scarves were visible against her flushed skin.

"What are you?" she finally managed.

I cradled her head against my chest, stroking the tangles from her hair.

"Whatever you want me to be."

Once she could stand and I was certain she wasn't going to pass out from what I'd done to her, I walked her back out to the rest of the club. We spent the next few hours together dancing arm in arm. When we finally parted, I could feel the lingering presence of her passion within me. Truly sated for the first time in what seemed like ages, I strode out into the night, the scent of Elizabeth still clinging to my flesh.

Seduction of a Swan

WARLOCK CORVIS NOCTURNUM

Dining? Alone, in this quiet, romantic little European restaurant so late?

Beg your pardon, m'Lady, how rude of me to approach unannounced. Please, allow me to introduce myself. My name is Amadeus. I am a vampire. I wasn't always a vampire, mind you. Once I was human, just like yourself, my scarlet haired vision. Hazy is my memory of it, distant like a dream. But what I do remember is that I was quite the lady's man.

Please, come, sit by me. I shall reveal to you my past, as I am lonely this starry night. Yes? Good. Now, where shall I begin…

Ah, the Age of Enlightenment! The pure brilliance of it all… it was the time of scientific discovery, when art and music flourished. The ballrooms filled to the brim with beautiful women in tight bodices, whose full breasts bulged to the point of spilling out, pardon me for being so blunt, m'Lady, but in truth, t'was the fad. If you believe the courtly days of old held no romance and heated passion you are wrong indeed. This was the time when Victorian romance novels would spring to life, inspiring lust in the hearts of the maidens, lovely young things who acted prim and proper in public, yet they read the works of the Marquis as hungrily as the young men, let me assure you.

It was shortly after arriving to my birthday party in the great hall of my ancestral home – manor, if you will – when as I greeted the guests I spotted a raven blue-black haired creature of unseen loveliness, decked out in a black and burgundy dress, a black lace choker around her neck with jewels nestling just above her ample bosom. Ah, she was pale and her eyes lost me in their green pools, as does yours! For a moment I thought you were she, only your hair is a radiant scarlet on milky white skin. I have not seen such beauty as yours since Miranda. See how you blush! It is adorable. Now where was I? Oh, yes, the birthday ball. As I reached my hand out to take hers to my mouth, I couldn't take my eyes off of hers. She seemed to hold me in her gaze, a smile upon her blood red lips as I lightly kissed her fingers. I must have held them longer that etiquette demanded of a lad in my station, for her coy smile and laugh – how I'll never forget her musical toned voice – asked if I was pleased with her presence. I inclined my head, in order to reply an affirmative, the words were simply lost on my tongue. Well, she was off in the crowd when one of my best friends, an artist named Byron came up to me. I smiled for I hadn't seen him for some days, in fact, it had been nearly a month of parties passed since. That wasn't like him at all, for Byron was a hedonist if ever there was one. He liked his ladies and young foppish lads too, if the truth be told! He wasn't like him to miss this and I was happy to take his arm.

'Were have you been?' I had scolded him with a mock reproach.

"Been sleeping in days, and having some wild nights,' he replied slyly. 'Do you like your gift I brought you?'

'Gift? I see no gifts,' I had replied.

'How rude of me! I brought you myself for one!' Byron leaned forward, winked and nodded to Miranda, 'And her as well.'

Well, needless to say I was dumbfounded. I couldn't believe my ears. A threesome with such an exquisite beauty, it was a dream come true, especially for a vibrant youth such as myself. I had laughed and hugged him, plying him with questions. Where had they meet, who exactly was she, I had wanted to know.

'All in due time. For now, enjoy the party,' was all he would say. He offered no explanations as to his whereabouts over the last month, but I could gather from Miranda's glances at my handsome friend and myself what was the story.

The hall was lit with candelabras and candles in great big fancy chandeliers, bathing the room in a warm soft glow. Several buffet tables covered in linens and crystal serving dishes dazzled the eye while a hidden orchestra played behind the lattice work, but amidst all the splendor all I could think of was her piercing eyes. A few hours later, after a few dances and toasts in my honor, I had to get some air.

Outside the draped doorway to the back half of the grounds I walked the stillness in the night air a stark contrast to the bright colors and mirth inside. The food had had little to stifle the emptiness inside me, and I needed to find solace in the dark. Not that I was unhappy over all mind you, I was rich, young, and attracted my share of women to my bed, but I had no real excitement in my life beyond my walled manor. In the shadows, however awaited a new life for me, yet I did not know until later that night that my birthday was to be my rebirth day.

Out of the shadows came Miranda's voice, low yet clear, 'might you want some company,' she asked.

"Yes, that would please me very much, 'I had said. In the dark it was easier not to be held by her gaze, but if you don't mind me saying, her ample cleavage was intoxicating in and of itself. How I desired her! She drew me to her and I could not help myself. I grasped her around the waist and pressed up against her.

'My, the birthday boy is excited by his gift,' she said, sliding a hand into my britches. The smile on her face widened as she realized the length and girth that met her fingers. She laughed, rich and deep, seductive and sweet as honey. Into the bushes we went, shedding clothes as we did. I removed my ruffled shirt and stopped, her naked upper half revealed, her dress spilling down around her. She put her hands on my belt and took it off, letting the leather pants drop with a skill so well practiced. My hardness swelled more, the breeze making me shiver.

'Let me warm you up,' she had said, pressing herself into me, her hardened nipples grazing my chest. I gasped as she took hold of me and with a deft motion of her fingers placed me between her thighs. We made love for what seemed like hours, heated and with energy unlike any other I'd ever known. Byron foot falls on the cobblestones around the corner foretold his coming. He smiled down at us, his shirt undone already.

The next hour seemed to last forever, with partners changing positions until she held me down and rode on top of me I panted, the pressure building. Miranda bit into my neck the endorphins masking the real pain, causing me to cry out, fluids began spurting hot. I felt faint, dizzy as never before. She gazed down at me, ebony locks curling to her nipples, a wicked smile on her lips. The shine on her lips was stained with blood, which she licked off seductively. She bit into her own wrist and trailed her arm across my lips, her large breasts touching me again.

'Drink,' she commanded. Without hesitation I did as asked, the realizing instantly Byron's reason for not coming out in the day lately had been two fold.

We traveled Europe for decades, relishing the sights and sounds of Paris, Italy, and more. The frolicking never grew old, but eventually Byron settled in the Americas, while

I remained with Miranda. She opened a few nightclubs in both counties, traveling back and forth by private jet at night. I rarely went with her but would occasionally ask of my old comrade's condition. I hear her has quite a name for himself now as a Gothic artist.

Ah, now, I see you eyes, you are convinced. My dear, Miranda would not mind if we indulged in our carnal appetites. In fact, I would think she would enjoy your accompanying me back to our sanctuary. Come, follow me.

I will lead you down a stone corridor to my bedchamber. Inside you'll see it is lavishly furnished like the Phantom of the Opera's lair. Sweeping open the door, I'll take you to a beautiful canopy bed, covered with soft black satin pillows. I will light the tapered candled and come up behind you. I lightly brush aside you hair from your shoulders. Slowly I'll run my hands down your neckline to the top of your dress, lowering your dress to your hips. The cool breeze will cause the candle light to flicker. A heavy drape gracefully will move as your head tilts backward. I'll place faint kisses on your neck, just behind your ear. Your nipples will harden ever so slightly, from the sensation of lips and wind outside. One hand grasps you about the lower back, my body presses into yours. I begin lowering my mouth to the back of your neck, teeth grazing the soft skin. You reach behind you; a hard lump pressed into your hip is growing longer. Slowly you'll trace your fingertips across it. My teeth press into your neck more firmly. Your breath will intake quickly, your breasts swell slightly and rise with desire. My other hand will trail my fingers down the side, sending shivers down your spine as I caress down your neck, feeling the softness of your skin. Lightly kissing the back of your shoulders, my hand will graze across your right nipple. You'll moan a bit louder, and your fingers will vainly try to grip my erection through my skintight leather trousers. It would be as if I would burst through the seams. I see you turning your head, looking up into my grey blue eyes, passion across my face. I'll open my mouth, and kiss you, softly at first, then more intently as you whimper and turn more, undoing my belt furiously. As my kisses grow stronger, your hands will pull down my pants. I'll break away briefly to give us both air. Panting a bit, I'll gently ease you onto the black swarm of pillows, inky as the night. It will be as if your luscious body is the glowing moon, the only light in my dark world. Your breasts will be heaving as I reach down, grasping your dress, pulling it down with urgency, a need that only you can fulfill. I can imagine your hair cascades across the bed, a mass of scarlet waves, shimmering in the candlelight. I'll rise above you, my hands along either side of your shoulders. Gazing into your beautiful eyes, I'll hesitate, and then descend downward, kissing you yet again with the same passion. My body will block the light in the room, dark waves of hair shadowing your vision. I will lower myself, kissing slowly down the side of your neck, across your shoulders. As I begin to kiss down your breasts, you'll bite your lip. My mouth grazes over a nipple, now protruding, waiting to be sucked. As I dance the tip of my tongue faintly over it, your hands will reach up and caress my shoulders, wanting more. I'll begin kissing a trail down your stomach, nearing your hips. You'll murmur and squirm, the sight of your delicious body writhing makes me shudder. You feel how hard I have become, as it touches your knee. It throbs, and I make a sound, vibrating your pubic hair. My tongue will dart across the warm opening; your hands tighten on my shoulders, fighting the urge to push my body downward, into you. I open my mouth; you feel the warm breath against your lips. I slowly descend and begin licking. Your eyes open wide now, as the feelings rush through you, a need builds. I'll run my hands down your body, caressing you as you moan. I look up at you, never stopping. Your eyes will not have closed again, lost in the intensity of it. Your hips'll move, as if they have a life all of their own, the dark sheets cause even more erotic sensations to run through you. I'll glide my hands down your side, nails grazing your breasts. You'll twitch. I tweak the nipples, your hips rise again. As your lower body rises, you'll grind against my tongue, my hands slide underneath you, gently cupping the roundness of your buttocks. I'll lean in a bit, working my mouth faster. After a few moments of this, you'll whisper, "Stop!"

And I'll pause, only long enough to rise up and drop down to lick your hard nipples. The tip of my erection will glide across your moist, hot folds, and you'll cry out. The heat from our passion will felt by us both. I'll put my hands under your shoulders, and begin kissing and biting softly at your neck.

Your head will then turn. Your mouth opens slightly, legs opening more. Your hips will rise as you try to fight the urge to grind against me. I smile, feeling the heat, the wetness. I'll push downward a bit, the pressure making you cry out. I'll bite down on the soft curve of where your neck and shoulder meet. Your hair, which smells sweet of petals, your skin glowing with the sheen of sweat. A cry of pleasure turns into an animal growl as I push slightly. The tip runs across your swollenness, begging to be filled. We'll keep going until you can stand it no more and ask me to take you.

Like me, you'll lose your hold on this mortal coil and walk the night and see it with new eyes.

The magic of the night will no longer all to you for you will be one with it. Forever.

THE ANIMAL AND THE DARKNESS

Michelle Belanger

I have always preferred the city at night. It never mattered which city. All cities, on one level or another are identical -- archetypal, even. This city was like all the others I have known. Follow a street far enough, and the rough bricks that pave it will grow rougher, the gaslights will grow farther and fewer between, and the darkness which lies at the heart of every city will gather together in one deep and luscious well. It is this darkness which attracts me invariably to any city. Daylight is the time of lies, when everyone is striving to convince everyone else that they lead good, kind, and chaste lives. The darkness is when the masks come down, when people are truly honest with themselves. Honesty appeals to me. Why pretend that we are not animals within?

This is the truth of things: At the heart of every city there is darkness and in the heart of every man there is an animal.

In this particular city these two elements came together in a delightful establishment known simply as "The Place." The Place was an exclusive club established by a local scion of the art community. Halaina Radenthall was a remarkable woman. She was the driving force behind most of the city's galleries, museums, and shows. A talented architect and interior designer, all of the city's most lavish and expensive buildings had been touched by her hand, shaped by her unique vision. Sensual, decadent, she made no pretensions by the light of day, though the good people of the city often sought to make them for her. No, Halaina knew that an artist's vitality arose from the creative impulse. The need to reproduce oneself in some fashion or another. Art for her was inextricably linked with sex. Considering the sensuous curves and erotic themes of the Art Nouveau style so popular then, it was surprising that the rest of the daylight culture did not actively acknowledge this connection as well. All one had to do was look closely at the lives of any artist of note at any point throughout history. Poets, painters, sculptors, writers -- all were libertines, all had appetites that the cultures which bred them openly shunned. But Halaina knew what the rest of the world had decided to overlook: Creativity was simply a symptom of an overactive libido. And so she created this wonderful Place where all manner of individuals of the artistic temperament could gather and indulge themselves.

The Place was, of course, a club of exclusive membership and only nominal legality. It was comparable to a high class bordello, but none of the patrons paid one another for their pleasure -- unless, of course, that was something they liked to do. The yearly membership fee was high enough to insure the presence of only the most serious of libertines and decadents. No one merely playing at perversion ever got in. The very location of The Place was kept in strictest secret. If you wanted to join, you had to wait for a member to approach you, and even then there was a careful screening process. All this caution was imperative considering the conservative atmosphere of the times. Poor Oscar Wilde had just been sentenced to hard labor for nothing but a little fling.

And Wilde's indiscretions were nothing compared to what went on at The Place. It was glorious. Halaina, brilliant as I've already said, not only understood human nature -- she celebrated it. Her grasp of the aesthetic, sensual, and decadent combined to make The Place into the haven of all earthly delights. Here were embraced all the varied aspects of that most fundamental human expression of creativity. The main lounge was equipped with a well-stocked bar and spacious dance floor. Tables were interspersed throughout, each lit with a delicate lamp of two long-fingered feminine hands cast in antiqued bronze holding a glowing, gas-lit orb. It was Halaina's work, designed from castings of her own hands -- hands known intimately by many patrons of The Place.

The Place was a testament to both Halaina's liberated vision of sensuality and her skill at interior design. The walls were covered with mirrors, each with acid-etched scenes of classical decadence. Nymphs clung to their sisters in sapphic embraces, and here and there a pair of smoothly etched thighs were spread for an intimate kiss. Satyrs with immense, uncircumcised members chased the almost child-like nymphs, who smiled coyly over their shoulders in encouragement, each figure crafted flawlessly by those self-same hands echoed upon every table. Gaslights fashioned to resemble calla lilies, those flowers whose very shape suggests coitus, sprouted at intervals from the walls. Everything was done in chrome and silver, occasionally accented with black -- Halaina's distinctive style of Art Nouveau already moving forward to the sleeker, sharper lines of Art Deco.

But the main room, glorious as it was, was only a front, really. It was designed to seem racy yet aesthetic so that the occasional inspection would reveal some truth to the rumors but nothing too offensive. The back rooms were the real delight and focus of The Place. Located behind well-secluded doors, a hallway stretched back into the depths of the building. It was lined with doors, each unimpressive in itself, almost utilitarian in appearance. Every door was outfitted with a secure lock. There were two keys to each of these locks. Halaina kept one. Robert Sorren, her long-time associate and maitre d' of The Place kept the other set. These were given out to patrons during the night as the need arose for more private and intimate quarters.

I had personally been to these rooms many times. Each had an immense four-poster bed with a full-length mirror located on the opposite wall, at least one couch, a dressing table, and an adjacent water closet. Two of the rooms were additionally outfitted with all manner of restraining devices. Eyelets were sunk securely into the walls, floors and ceilings. Chains and manacles could be attached to any of these. There was a sturdy St. Andrew's Cross built against one wall and a pole, running from the ceiling to the floor and outfitted with eyelets was located several feet beyond the foot of the bed. A very intricate saw-horse affair, upholstered in rich leather and outfitted with a number of findings and straps, occupied one corner in lieu of a chair. Chests against the walls contained a wide variety of whips, scourges, riding crops, gags, chastity belts, dildos, and plugs -- most designed by long-time member Richard Dunhurst, the local bondage aficionado and owner of the city's largest chain of hardware stores.

I am not as intimately acquainted with the particular contents of the other rooms since the bondage rooms -- suites number 5 and 7-- were my particular favorites. However, I do recall that most of the rooms had a semi-secret space in between them where those of voyeuristic tastes could avail themselves of the peepholes. In all, the rooms allowed for any manner of indulgence a creative soul could devise. All in a secure and private place, almost completely soundproofed, and surrounded by others who shared the same delights and desires.

I procured a membership almost as soon as I came to the city and made a point of attending The Place at least once a week. Fridays were always a little too busy for my tastes. It was so hard to make a selection from among the other members and then the wait for the rooms was interminable. I preferred Sunday nights. It was the Lord's day of rest, after all. At least I appreciated the irony. And, though there were fewer patrons sipping champagne at the tables or dancing to the exotic music of Halaina's performers, there was never any shortage of choices.

I preferred my women small-boned and breakable: large-eyed frail beauties with a long rope of hair that could be used as a leash or pulled tightly around the throat whenever required. Submissives were easy to find. Even those women with enough will to overcome the moral conditioning of the age could rarely rise above their designation as the "weaker sex." Which was just fine with me. My favorite was Marguerite. She was the daughter of a wealthy local family, and I was certain it would have killed her parents to know that a portion of their prestigious old money bought her long nights of degrading sex all year long. She seemed innocent enough, though she was renowned for her appetite. I liked both the innocence and the appetite. It was like corrupting her all over again each time.

I recall one night in the late spring of '98. Marguerite was there with her sometime lover, Elizabeth. Both of the women were fond of very tight corsets. Elizabeth had a stunning 14 inch waist, and Marguerite, at 15 inches, was always struggling to outdo her. The results were always appealing. I never quite understood how the two of them worked as lovers, however. Both were inveterate submissives and loved to be fucked long and hard with as large a member as they could get between their thighs. Though I never looked in on one of their sessions together, I got great amusement from imagining them lying naked together on one of the great, wide beds, each caressing the aromatic flesh between her friend's thighs and whispering fantasies that were anything but Sapphic.

When Marguerite caught sight of me, she waved me over immediately. "Nathaniel!"

"Good evening, ladies. Enjoying yourselves?" I sat down and motioned for a drink. Halaina stocked the best absinthe in town.

Elizabeth pouted a little and shrugged. "I don't know why I keep coming here on Sunday nights. There's never anyone I like."

"I would be more than happy to entertain you," I offered, "but I know I'm a little too refined for your tastes."

She shrugged. "I know what I like. I want a man who can make me feel forced to obey him. He has to take his pleasure whether I will it or no." She leaned in closer to Marguerite and myself, her eyes gleaming. "I like my men brutish, rough. Hairy, with thick arms and legs, and a thick cock to go with them. I want an animal, Nathaniel, not a boy." She sat back a little, making a dismissive gesture with one hand. "You're too thin and you're more boy than man. Don't take it the wrong way. You're very attractive, but for me it's the kind of beauty you admire in a Greek statue. It's to be appreciated from afar -- not fucked in a dark bedroom in a tangle of sweaty sheets."

I smiled. "I assure you I'm much older than I look -- "

"So you've said -- "

"-- But I accept the compliment for what I know it's worth. You know what I like in a woman, Elizabeth. And I like it precisely because I can force her and break her to my will. Those little sounds of passion someone makes when you have forced them to experience pleasure beyond anything they dreamed themselves capable of -- those are my most precious music, my sweetest wine." I sipped the absinthe, savoring its bitter bite on my tongue. Marguerite looked on in silence, and I could see by her flushed cheeks that she was recalling vividly some of that precious music which had escaped her own throat only a few weeks before. I turned to her.

"So." I stroked her cheek with one long finger then grasped her tiny pointed chin in my hand. I brought her head around to me, forcing her chin up so we locked eyes. "I already have the key to suite number five. I spoke with Richard the other day and he has repaired that gag you like so well. The one you almost bit through," I reminded, giving her chin a sharp squeeze. She looked deliciously repentant. "Shall we?"

She nodded silently, her eyes locked on mine. She knew I would tolerate nothing but obedience in this. I had trained her very well.

"If you will excuse us, then, Elizabeth," I said, finishing off the rest of the absinthe and getting to my feet. I grabbed the black satin choker Marguerite wore at her throat. From experience I knew it was much sturdier than it looked. "You," I punctuated it with a yank on the choker. "Come with me."

I marched her back to the fifth suite. I had already seen to the preparation of the room. A faint scent of incense was noticeable in the hall as we approached.

"Tell me what you want me to do to you," I whispered, leaning my face into her soft, fragrant hair.

She paused in front of the door as I unlocked it. I maintained a nominal hold on the choker at her throat.

"I want you to make me want it," she whispered huskily. "I want you to tease me and play with me until I can't stand it any longer. I want you to make me beg you to fuck me. Like I'll die or go mad if you don't."

I pulled her closer to me, pressing her body against mine. I took her face in both of my hands and held it so that she could not look away from me. I stared hard into her hazel eyes.

"Do you want me to make you feel the animal?" I asked softly, holding my face close to hers so my lips nearly caressed her skin.

She nodded.

"At home, I have to pretend to be chaste and good," she pouted. "I'm not allowed to say that I want anything. I'm not allowed to feel. Good girls don't touch that place between their thighs. Good girls don't get wet when they think about men -- good girls don't even think about men and what they can do to them! I want you to force that on me. Make me want you so badly I can't pretend not to! Make me want to touch myself or scream because I can't. I want to be consumed with wanting you, so there's nothing, nothing in me but want!"

I held her face a little more tightly in my hands and my voice grew very, very soft, so she felt more than she heard the words.

"You want me to summon your darkest, most desperate desire." She nodded against my hands, her eyes rapt. "You want me to bring out the animal in you, to make you feel nothing but lust. The dark well which you want me to explore in you -- " I paused, savoring memories of past encounters. With a bittersweet sigh, I rasped, "The emotions that can be dredged out of it are very potent, my dear. They are not things to be toyed with. Once you take them out, you can't always put them back again. Do you really want me to do that to you?"

Her eyes glistening with fear and desire, she nodded.

I pulled her face against mine, resting my cheek against hers. I could feel her skin flush beneath mine. I rested my lips almost against her ear, so each warm breath rustled the tiny hairs there.

"Then I promise you that tonight will change you forever. Tonight I will bring out the animal and the darkness, and you will know that they are a part of you. You will have no choice but to accept them. They will consume you. Utterly."

I abruptly let her go and stepped past her, opening the door. She almost fell into the space I had occupied but a moment ago. Her eyes were closed, and there was an expression of intense anticipation on her face. I stood just inside the door for a moment, waiting for her to follow me in.

I had turned the gaslights on very low, so their light did not illuminate the room so much as they served to define the shadows. The bed had a very sturdy mahogany frame. Like everything else Halaina kept in The Place it was a perfect marriage of both form and function. Thick, carved posts rose up to a canopy frame overlaid with a sheer, wispy material. The eyelets anchored into the posts were almost unnoticeable, as were those located in the canopy frame above the foot and head of the bed. The bed was covered with pillows and rich coverlets. The whole was done in deep reds and gold, which accented nicely the black leather restraints Richard so lovingly crafted. I threw Marguerite onto the bed and shut the door, drawing the inside bolt.

"Well then. We shall begin without ado," I told her, taking off my jacket and setting it on a chair. "Come here."

She stood and approached me. Her golden-haired head came up barely past my shoulder. Her face was pallid in the dim gaslight, and her dark eyes drank in the shadows.

"What do you want me to do?" she asked quietly. There was a slight tremble to her voice. Her hands were restless, running lightly up and down my chest, probing for my nipples through my shirt.

"Turn around."

She did and I began to undress her. I took my time, carefully undoing the long string of buttons that fastened her dress. When the dress and petticoats lay pooled around her ankles, I began on the corset. This amazing piece of women's apparel was much sturdier and allowed for much rougher treatment. I yanked Marguerite's thin little body around as I loosened the tight web of strings that had blessed her with her

15 inch waistline. Finally I had it off and set it aside on the chair with my jacket. Marguerite gasped a little, now that her breathing was less restricted. I turned her around to face me. She had high, round breasts, more than ample when unfettered by the corset. The nipples were a dark pink, tight and erect with rather small aureoles I could cover with two fingers each. Her skin, always demurely covered from the light of the sun, was very pale, and it glowed like flawless marble in the gaslight.

I loosened her hair and it fell in a long golden sheath down her back. A bit of ribbon, and it became the perfect leash or choker or whatever I willed. I caught up a handful near the nape of her neck and pulled her head tightly back. A tiny gasp escaped her lips. I kissed them, briefly, then ran my lips and tongue down her cheek, to the hollow of her jaw, lingering briefly along the length of her neck where I could feel her pulse, fast and hard, just beneath the flesh. I held her head back tightly while I explored the hollows around her collarbone, then traced the rondure of each breast. Her nipples had clenched like tiny little fists by this point, and I took the right one up into my mouth, rolling it between my lips then biting with my teeth. I sucked on it long and hard, pressing my chin into the cushion of her breast. I pressed my free hand against the crotch of her bloomers, pleased with the building heat I could feel there.

I broke away suddenly, pulling her nipple in my teeth a little. She rewarded me with a little cry. I twisted her around by her hair and marched her back over to the bed. With my free hand, I divested her of her bloomers, so she stood, naked except for the black satin choker at her throat.

"Open your mouth," I said, taking the gag out from beneath one of the pillows. It was a thick piece of black leather with a tongue-shaped bit protruding from the inside. I pushed the bit into her mouth until the leather was flush to her lips. Then I lifted her hair and buckled the gag into place, pulling it shut as tightly as her flesh would allow.

Marguerite looked up at me with her huge, innocent eyes. I smiled wickedly.

"Not this time," I told her. "You can beg more loudly with those eyes than you can with your voice anyway." I produced a blindfold from underneath the same pillow. Marguerite looked a little distressed as I fastened this tightly around her head, but her breath came more quickly.

"Put out your hands."

I looped a long strip of deep purple silk around her wrists, crossing it once and pulling it through the space beneath her hands. When her hands were secure, I took the ends of the silk and wound them once around her upper arms, crossing them at her back. Her little fists were pressed tightly between her breasts, and her upper arms pushed her breasts together, highlighting them nicely. I brought the length of silk back around to her front, fastening it again at her wrists.

"That should do. For now."

I slid a hand between each breast and forearm, lifting it up a little and making sure that it rested neatly in the crook of her elbow. Her nipples shone hard and dark on either side of her wrists. She made a few noises into the gag, but a swift yank on her hair silenced her protests.

I paused a bit to survey my handiwork, rather absently rolling her nipples between my fingers. Bondage is an artform, and any body can be used as a canvas, but the results are especially pleasing when you have a quality canvas to work from. I approved of Marguerite's form.

"Lie down."

I didn't wait for her to comply, just shoved her down onto the bed. While she recovered, I bent down and reached under the bed. My hand closed around the apparatus I sought.

"Spread your legs," I told her as I brought up a long, metal pipe with two manacles attached at either end. It was actually two pipes, one nested inside the other, and fixed in the middle so the whole could be widened or shortened in length. I went to the foot of the bed and set the pipe lengthwise between her ankles. "Wider," I said, not quite pleased with the result. She lifted her head in my direction, making a querying noise from under her gag.

"Don't question me," I cautioned her, grabbing a handful of her pubic hair and giving it a warning pull. "Just do it."

She stretched her legs as far as they would go. Her ankles almost reached to the edges of the bed. I leaned over and began fastening her legs to the pipe, pulling the manacles tightly around her dainty ankles. I paused a moment for her to test the results. She wiggled her hips a little and tried bringing her legs together. The manacles allowed a little give, and then they encountered the pole. She pressed her ankles against it with a little more force, and quickly realized that her legs were going to stay spread. She tried bringing her knees together, but her legs were too widely splayed. I reached down and extended the pole another few inches, forcing her legs apart even farther.

"How do you like that? It's Richard's work, so it's going to hold. You can wiggle and squirm against it all you want. I pulled the manacles tight -- all the way to the last hole. You've got tiny little feet and I wouldn't want you pulling loose."

She struggled experimentally and gave up with an exasperated sound. For a moment, she turned her attention to the bonds at her wrists, but I didn't give her a chance to work on that.

"That's only temporary," I said, rolling her over onto her belly. With the pole between her legs it was easy, all I had to do was twist it in the middle and she had to follow it around. "On your knees."

The pole splayed her legs at an unaccustomed angle, and so she was a little shaky, but she eventually managed to get to her knees on the bed. She faced the head of the bed blindly, tossing her head a little to get all of her hair to fall in one direction.

I moved silently across the room to the water closet. The water basin still had pieces of ice floating in it. It hadn't melted completely since I put it there. That was good. It meant I could use the ice along with what I had chilled in the ice water. I removed the two-pronged device and toweled it off a bit at the base so I could fastened it back onto its belt. I applied a liberal dose of scented oil to both prongs. It was very cool against my hand, and I avoided touching it as much as possible so my body heat wouldn't warm it up. I took up the belt and snapped the apparatus into place. Then I took the second part of the belt and approached Marguerite. I laid everything down on the edge of the bed, then pushed her forward. She fell on her face in the pillows, her golden hair spilling all over the place. Her ass was up in the air, and I blew lightly on the pink flesh it exposed. Somewhere in the depths of the pillows, Marguerite moaned softly.

"You think you know what's coming, don't you?" I taunted. I took up the first belt, specially sized because of her waist. "You think you have me all figured out."

I wound the first belt around her waist and buckled it tightly into place. She seemed a little confused. I had never used this particular piece of equipment on her, but I was eager to observe the results.

"What is that, you ask? Why did I put a belt on you? Whatever could be going on?" I slapped her on the ass and then got up on the bed behind her. This seemed to be familiar territory to her. I ran my hand along her sex, stroking her labia open and teasing the lips of her vagina. She was slick and fragrant, with a sweet scent like honeyed musk. I preferred Marguerite to a number of other women at The Place for this reason. She was always a pleasure to taste and her scent, even at its most animal, was always sweet like perfume.

I played with the petalled layers of moist flesh. She gasped at the first few touches; my fingers were still cool from the ice water. But her heat soon warmed them up. When her lips opened to me of their own accord, I slid a finger in, running it around shallowly on the inside of her. As I judged her response and readiness, I shoved it in deep and hard, wiggling against the slick, hot flesh inside. She cried out behind the gag, tossing her shoulders and struggling against the pillows.

"Here's familiar territory," I whispered against her. She felt the words even if she did not hear them. I held each of her round, white buttocks in my hands as I studied her sex. Finally, I bent and kissed her, probing her layers with my tongue, teasing mostly, savoring the rich sweetness of her as it mingled with the lingering taste of wormwood on my tongue. I kissed her a little more deeply, gripping her thighs and pulling her into me. My tongue reached deep inside of her, and I strained to lick against the walls of her. Marguerite had turned her head on its side in the pillows, and her golden hair lay in streams across her face. Her cheeks were flushed a deep pink and her breath came in quick little gasps. Not stopping my work with my tongue, I reached behind me with one hand and took up the two-pronged apparatus. It was still quite cool to the touch, especially in comparison to the growing heat against my mouth. I reached around with my other hand and braced my forearm against her hips. She tried to grind her pubis against my wrist. I smiled and, pulling my mouth slowly away from her, positioned the prongs just outside of her cunt and her puckered little asshole.

She jumped as I slowly pressed the chilled prongs against her warm flesh. I let them rest lightly against her, so she could get used to it and really think about what was going to happen to her. Then I began to press ever so gently, moving the dildos in a circular motion to get her to open up for me. The flesh around her asshole quivered a little, and I smiled as I thought of the unexpected chill that sill clung to both prongs of the dildo. I pressed a little, and the lips of her vagina parted to accept the thick, rounded head of the first prong. Her ass still resisted, but I was beginning to make headway. She had taken things in her ass before. In fact, I knew she rather liked it, though I also knew she had never had anything quite so large. She really didn't go for out and out sodomy, though a finger or a tongue were always welcome.

Finally she began opening up and I slowly slid everything in. I imagined her eyes behind the blindfold getting wider and wider as she was filled up more and more. I took things in stages, and she caught her breath each time I pushed the dildos a little further in. The dildos were rather wide at the base, and it was pleasing to watch her flesh open up around them. Only an inch or so remained, but things were thick enough that her labia and buttocks were forced wide in an effort to hold it all. She was holding her breath, now, focused completely on being filled. The only sound in the room was the wet noise of the dildos churning against her flesh as I moved them around and coaxed her to take it all.

When I was satisfied that she had taken as much as she would hold, I brought the back strap up between her cheeks and fastened it in place on the belt around her waist. When this was snug, I yanked a little needlessly on the front strap as I brought it around against her pubis and fastened it to the other side of the waist-belt. I pulled the buckle to the last possible notch watching Marguerite writhe and twist and the dildos were driven even further into the depths of her. With the belt fastened and the dildos locked in place, Marguerite thrashed on the bed, crying out and straining against the gag. The cold, the length, the sudden fullness within her -- I held her hips firmly and pressed my hand against the base of the belt, wiggling the apparatus around and smiling at her reaction.

"Do you like that?" I asked her, pressing my hand against the base of the apparatus and moving it around a little. The noises she made were answer enough. Again I used the pole between her legs to force her to roll over. Her hair was a tangled around her face and neck, a few long gold strands catching between her fingers and bound wrists. She grunted a little when her ass settled on the bed and drove the dildos home at a slightly different angle.

I took a second length of purple silk and fastened it around the middle of the pole. I threaded the other end through an eyelet in the canopy frame above the foot of the bed and hoisted her legs into the air. When they were positioned to my liking, I knotted it securely. Then I bent to her wrists and began undoing the first temporary bond. Her breasts were a little too tempting in this position, caught as they were between her arms, and so I paused before undoing the knot to bite and lick and suck at each nipple, testing the amount of pressure I could apply with my teeth before she gasped or cried out through the gag. Then I loosened the silk. She flexed her fingers and rotated her wrists, then ran her hands over her own breasts, playing with nipples made tender by my attentions. I slid the silk out from under her and let it drop to the floor. Then I reached above her to the right-hand post and brought the manacle there out from underneath the covers. I grabbed her wrist and pulled it back, stretching her arm until her wrist met the manacle. I was a little rough, and she whimpered in protest, rolling her head from side to side and turning her head to where she thought I was.

"You don't have your eyes to plead with," I reminded her, jerking the other arm back and fastening it to the other manacle. "You can't beg and I won't stop. I've filled you up, but the dildos are strapped tight to you. You can grind a little, but with your legs spread this far, I doubt it will do you any good. All it's meant to do it tease you." I planted a hand between her thighs and ground it into her. "How do you like it inside of you? I've fucked you before. I know how much you can hold. I picked this one out especially for you. You should be filled near to bursting."

She nodded, making a tiny, almost pitiful sound in the back of her throat.

"I don't think you've ever had anything this big in your ass before. Do you like it? Do you?" She nodded again, grinding her hips against my hand. With her legs spread apart and suspended, she couldn't get much purchase, so I know she was disappointed with the result. I placed a finger against the base of the back prong and vibrated it slightly. When she moaned, I increased the speed and pressure, then, as she began to breathe hard and toss her head, I withdrew unexpectedly. She made an impatient little noise, so I brought my hand hard down against one thigh. The resulting crack of flesh against flesh echoed throughout the room. She made a more appropriate noise, so I kissed the reddened flesh where I had slapped her.

"Good girl," I whispered. "You know how to behave -- and you know what happens when you don't." I began undressing myself, stripping down to my shorts. I knelt on the bed beside her and bent down to her breasts. I began a slow exploration of the tender undersides of her breasts with my mouth and tongue, pausing occasionally to speak. "I'm the one in charge here. I decide when it will hurt and when it will feel good." I lightly pressed my hand against the strap between her thighs. "And I decide whether or not you get to come."

She whimpered at that, but I ignored it. Instead, I focused my attention upon the soft flesh of her breasts and belly, exploring with lips and teeth and tongue the sensitive regions around her hips, her tender sides, and beneath each outstretched arm. She twitched and quivered beneath my touch, moaning and writhing in her restraints. My own pleasure lay in watching her achieve hers, and so I had no need to rush these proceedings. I could feel the desire building within her, along with the frustration. In manifested itself in a flush not only in her face but across her breasts as well. The pulse in her neck was visible through the skin, and the beating of her heart vibrated her ribcage in counterpoint to her rapid breathing. She was warm everywhere, but was particularly radiating heat from her strapped-up nether regions. A slight sheen of sweat had begun to show between her breasts, under her arms, and just inside her thighs. The room was redolent with the spicy-sweet scent of her lust. Nothing could have been more delicious.

I continued to taste and tease her flesh -- touching her everywhere but the most desired areas. Her nipples and her cunt I left alone, ignoring the way she lifted her hips to entice me or shook her torso back and forth so her breasts slid heavily from side to side.

I am a strong believer that the most agonizing torture has nothing to do with pain but with the with-holding of pleasure. Many years of experience have only served to prove this in my mind. I consider myself a talented lover, and I always tailor my love-making to the particular tastes of my partner, but this one thing I never alter. Desire only feeds itself with its hunger, and so the more protracted a climax can be made, the more intense the end result inevitably will be.

When I felt that she had suffered enough, I began to unstrap the double-pronged belt I had buckled so securely into her flesh. She had given up trying to grind against it long ago, learning all too quickly that such action only frustrated her more. Exhausted with arousal, she simply lay against the bed, her breathing quick yet even, waiting for me to free her. The completest submission. Now it was time.

I ground the dildos into her a little, playing with the various reactions different angles, depths, and rhythms received. Then I slid the apparatus out with a slow, protracted motion, compensating each time she writhed or thrust her hips. I set the thing aside near the foot of the bed. Her scent, heady, rich, and a little sharp with her need, flooded into the room, and I knelt back between her legs, just drinking it in. I blew a little on her sex. It was moist and red and swollen, and each time she raised her hips in my direction, the lips of it sucked at the air as it they could pull it in and fill themselves. I slid out of my shorts, stroking myself gently. I ran a finger along her innermost lips and rubbed the slickness against my glans. She gasped and shuddered at my touch, anticipating that an end to her suffering was near at hand.

Instead of thrusting into her immediately, I brought my finger back and began to play with her, splaying open the wet red folds of flesh and stroking her clitoris. The motion was slow at first, but I increased the speed until I was almost vibrating against her flesh. She rewarded me with the prettiest bout of writhing I had seen in a while, twisting her shoulders and her hips and rolling herself against me. She made gentle, urgent noises in the back of her throat but was careful to keep them free of any sound of impatience or pleading. She knew exactly where that would get her.

She thought that she could not get aroused any further. She thought that her body could not sustain any more pleasure without achieving some sort of release. I proved to her otherwise, taking her above the plateau she had achieved and taking her higher and higher. I could feel every muscle inside her with my tongue. Everything was taut and tense and strumming and ready to explode. I sucked on her labia and pressed my tongue against her clitoris, licking it swiftly and gently again and again until she screamed into her gag and her entire body was wracked with throes of a pleasure that was still not truly a release.

She lay, tossing her head back and forth on the pillow, sending her golden hair cascading everywhere. I laughed. From the lines of her jaw and the bulging of the muscles there, she was lucky she had the gag to bite down on; she might have shattered teeth otherwise. There is no keener torture than pleasure that has passed beyond all previous boundaries of sensation. With that thought, I plunged into her for the first time, and felt her hot, rippling flesh grip me invitingly. She tried to grind into me, but again the way her legs were suspended prevented her from doing this adequately. Instead, she just lay back, panting, waiting for me to plunge into her again and again. I slid my whole length slowly in and out, teasing her with the tip before entering. Then I slowly increased my rhythm, carefully feeling the minute tensings and movements in the flesh within her. I wanted to time things just right --

I sped up, plunging hard into her, over and over again. Each thrust vibrated through the flesh of her breasts, and her head was thrust deeper into the pillows. She was making a rhythmic noise beneath the gag, somewhere between a moan and a whimper. The sound matched the rhythm of my thrusts. Then I felt her insides tense around me, as the first preliminary shudder began to hit --

And I withdrew. Completely. Suddenly. It took her a moment to realize what had happened. Then she threw her head back violently into the pillows and screamed her frustrations out into the gag. I watched with a wicked smile on my lips. She thrashed furiously in her bonds, no longer the docile little innocent who so placidly allowed me to tie her up. Now she wanted her freedom, wanted to loose her legs and churn her thighs and bring her hands down to touch the fire that had almost ignited in her loins.

"Marguerite," I said and was ignored. I tapped her belly, just above her pubis. "Marguerite."

She paused in her thrashing and turned her blind face toward me.

"Count with me."

She screamed and thrashed, grinding her hips into the air.

"Count with me," I persisted, laying a finger on her belly. "One ..."

She was trying to speak through the gag, but only grunts and growls came out. They were deliciously bestial. She was all beast now, nothing but pure, animal need. She knew nothing of counting. I was going to make her wait, tottering on that edge, to count? Her rage was beautiful.

"Count with me, Marguerite. One, two ... " I pause for several breaths. She tossed her head and tried to utter "three" through the gag. "Three," I acknowledged. "Four, five ..."

I drew it out as long as I could, pausing longer and longer between numbers. When I reached each number, I placed another finger onto her belly, so she could feel it. "Nine. Ten," I said laying the pinky of my left hand down on her flesh. She started nodding her head rapidly, urging me to begin where I had so unexpectedly left off. "Eleven," I said and was rewarded anew with all manner of screams and thrashings.

After an agonizing count of fifteen, I thrust back into her suddenly. She received me with open, all-consuming lust. Inside, she sucked at me with muscles she had probably always ignored. Until now. I pounded into her and felt her build again, this time far more rapidly. Her voice was a little ragged behind the gag now, her throat raw from her furious protestations. I felt the inside of her clench around me like a fist, and I increased the rhythm and depth. Then the first few tremors began to ripple around me, and it was all I could do to stay inside her as the thrashed and writhed and ground and screamed. Her desire, so drawn out and tense, had hung almost palpably on the air, and now her climax rang throughout the room. I could feel it washing over me like a tidal wave, carrying me out to the depths with her. Only when that pleasure -- primal, mystical, transformative in its intensity -- broke against me did I climax as well, caught up completely in the furious, all-consuming pleasure that wracked her flesh.

When the last wave had shattered against us, and she trembled beneath me making tiny, strangled noises in the back of her throat, I finally withdrew. She shuddered along the whole length of me, gasping when she found herself empty. Then she lay perfectly still upon the bed, overcome by the depths that she did not suspect she had possessed. I stretched out on the bed beside her but did not untie her quite yet. I regarded her legs, stretched out above the bed. The muscles deep in her thighs were trembling visibly. I ran a finger along the inside of one thigh and Marguerite uttered a gasp that was almost a scream. I brought my hand to the base of her thigh. She weakly shook her head "no", but I proceeded anyway. I searched through the hot, sticky folds of her flesh and found her clitoris again. My finger stroked it slowly, relentlessly. I could feel her pulse down there, the rhythm hard and deep. She whimpered but seemed to pass beyond even non-verbal noises after that, as I took the last ripples of pleasure and drew them out even further, until she was nothing but one tightly strung nerve that vibrating each time I touched it. When I had exhausted the last possible shred of sensation, lowered her legs to the bed. I loosed her wrists and her ankles, then just lay with my fingers tangled in the dark blond curls of her nether hair. She dozed a while, and I listened as her heartbeat slowed to a more sedate pace.

After we had rested and washed up in the water closet, I helped Marguerite back into her clothes. She underwent the proceedings in complete, almost stunned silence. The lacing of the corset was almost another bout of bondage in and of itself. To get it as tight as she liked it, she had to hold onto the post of the bed and brace her feet against the floor while I planted a hand firmly in the middle of her back and pulled on the laces with the other. Finally, corseted to her liking, I fastened the long string of tiny buttons that went up the back of her dress.

Her face was still flushed even now, and her eyes burned with a light and a knowledge that had not been there before. She had touched the animal, had been the animal completely for perhaps the first time. The weight of that, the memory, the realization that the ravenous beast was still her, even in its manic raging -- perhaps her eyes were no longer innocent, but I found them all the more appealing.

SILENT ECHOES

by Mora Zoranokov

He was quiet tonight, sitting alone at a window overlooking a nearly deserted street. The sky churned with clouds, brightened slightly by the moon they concealed. The rain wasn't heavy; could stop at any moment. Yet it had fallen like this all day and well into the night. *"How did it come to this?"* he asked himself silently as his gaze dropped from the window. His eyes slid closed for a moment, and there she was, in the deep recesses of his thoughts. She had been there for years now, but he had never fully understood to what extent. She had been the one to comfort him when his wife was slain. She had been there to right his mind when he began to doubt himself, and slip towards insanity. To the rest of the world, she could appear cold as lifeless marble, but not to him. With him her hands were gentle, and her eyes understanding. He hated it that she saw him in such a weakened state, but she never once turned him away when he needed her. Two years had passed, and he still felt the guilt from his former lover's death. But even when she had been busting skulls all night to get her point across to her deaf superiors, she would still take him into her arms. He had strengthened since Angelique's death, and she saw it in him, clear as the moon on a cloudless night. Spark by spark, his soul was beginning to rekindle. In the back of his mind he heard the prince's words again. His fists clenched and trembled. How could the prince be such a fool in the face of such clear and present danger? He turned from the window before the urge to smash it could take over his senses. *"Fuck it"*, he thought. *"It's the prince's mess, let him deal with it."*

He had passed her room and tilted his head towards the door, drawing in a breath through his nose. She wasn't there. He sighed, a little disappointed, and continued his aimless journey through. He left the apartment and slipped into the alleyway behind it and paced like a rabid hound, unsure of what to do. Scenes of their times together began to play in his mind. The many nights on the bar deck, the nights they would walk the property line together. His pacing slowed as another memory came to his mind, the night they lay beneath the moonlight on a warm summer night by the lakeside. Had he dreamed that night? His eyes clenched a little as he sought to divide reality from fantasy. Had she really kissed him? He shook his head with a guttural snarl. *"No"*, he thought as his pacing increased in tempo, *"that couldn't have happened."*

As he passed through another alleyway, a low, almost hushed voice followed him:

"It's seems inevitable. The moon shall rise, the hands of time keep marching onward, and the dismal soul that is my brother shall be restless once again."

Guevarden stopped as the voice caught his ear and he turned, crossing his arms over his chest as he peered at the younger Gangrel. Gaelyn sat very nonchalantly on the edge of a packing crate, a copy of Tolkien's "The Silmarillion" in his hands. His eyes had not yet pulled from the pages.

"Gaelyn, you're twenty four years old, why do you have to talk like your Othello's Leiutenant?"

Gaelyn finally looked up at his older brother and smiled.

"Cassio identified that without his good name, he was nothing but a beast. If only all our bretheren could be so wise." His hands closed the book softly as he stood. "Tell me brother, what worries fuel you this night?" A frown slowly formed over his face. "And if you tell me that you're stressing about what the prince said, I'll disassemble that precious car of yours piece by piece." He grinned, preparing to be smacked.

The elder brother simply looked away and shook his head.

"I don't know, kid. Something is just… gnawing at my mind."

Gaelyn's eyes widened. He had just threatened Guevarden's car. His most prized possession, a gift from his wife, and he hadn't even batted an eyelash! He had seen lesser men beaten to a bloody pulp for such words. Gaelyn was no fool though, and he had his suspisions. He paced around behind his brother and whispered a single word to him…"Winter."

Guevarden spun at his brother and glared at him, a snarl coming to his lips.

"What of her?"

Gaelyn remained calm. He had seen his brother snarl and snap at him countless times before. He smiled a little. It was interesting to see how much alike they really were. He sighed as he looked up to Guevarden's face before continuing.

"Sometimes I really pity you, Guevarden. You're stronger than I, faster than I. You have an exotic look that intrigues most females. But even though your eyes are more interesting to behold than mine, it is I who have the clearer vision. You are so blind that you cannot see the obvious. I doubt you would see it if it was tattooed right to the end of your nose."

Guevarden's brows knit a little and his head cocked to one side, much like a dog's.

Again Gaelyn sighed. He shook his head in disbelief.

"I'll use small words for you, oh thick headed one." He looked Guevarden right in the eyes. "You're in love with her."

Guevarden pulled back from Gaelyn, stunned. The words hit him like a bullet in the chest. Memories of how she made him feel began to flood his senses at a rapid pace. Gods on high, he was right. The elder turned from the younger and paced off, leaving Gaelyn to return to his reading spot, content that his older brother may finally have found a reason to live again.

~*~*~*~*~*~*~

"Up against the wall, bitch." The command was barked into her ear as she was shoved roughly against the exterior of the club she had just exited. Her eyes closed and took in the scent. There were two men and both reeked of cigarettes and wet stale sweat.

"No, please… don't." Her voice trembled.

"Just keep your goddamned mouth closed." His body pressed against hers and held her to the wall. Winter nearly choked on his stench as it assaulted her nose. To make it worse, he had tried to cover his filth with cheap cologne. His hands roved her body.

"My… my purse… it's..." He ripped it from her hand and pressed her face against the wall as his hand groped her crotch. She sucked in a sharp breath involuntarily.

"Mm. You like this? You're a hot little bitch, aren't you?" His breath was worse than the rest of him. "Come on, baby, let me know you're not dead!"

"What do you want me to say?" she stammered. Her assailant spun her around and shoved her back against the wall, his hand firmly around her throat. She could feel the brick snagging at her skin and clothes as he forced her to her knees.

His friend spoke up. "I like tall girls. You know what I like them to do for me?"

She gulped. "N-n-no."

The first man ran his thumb over her cheek. "Baby, you can't be a day over eighteen. I know you have to be legal since you were dancing in the club there." His crotch brushed against her face. "You know what I want from you?"

She squeaked in response.

The companion knelt down beside her, his face in hers. "Cry for me."

"You don't want me to do that."

The standing man struck her hard across the cheek. "Don't you fucking tell me what I want, you fucking bitch!" His free hand fumbled with his jeans. He unzipped and unbuttoned them, exposing his dick. "You're going to tell me that I have the biggest cock you've ever seen."

"Actually," her voice was suddenly calmed, collected, and very snide. "I would have to say that you're rather small." He raised his hand and struck at her again, this time she caught his wrist in her hand. She squeezed his wrist and yanked him off balance. Winter stood and slammed her fist into the wall beside her, powdering the facing. She blew the dust from her knuckles and admired the quarter inch dent it had left in the stucco. Her gaze leveled with the two men as they tremored before her. "So. Which one of you wants to be first?" Standing transfixed, the would-be muggers said nothing and did not take their eyes off of her. Winter's posture drooped and she leaned back against the wall. Folding her arms across her chest, she shook her head and clucked. "You know something? Muggers just aren't what they used to be. Go ahead. Run. It'll be funny." The two men ran at breakneck speed down the alleyway. Winter smiled and shook her head. She propped her foot against the wall behind her. The lead up and the chase were her favorite parts. She waited until they were nearly to the street, about ten yards away from her, before moving.

Winter plucked them up from the ground and was back to the spot where they had begun their flight before either of them knew what hit them. She deposited them against the ground and waited for the realization to sink in. Their eyes grew wide and they paled slightly. She smirked at them. They were off again, running down the alleyway in the opposite direction. She waited, again, until they were nearly to the street. This time it was about fifteen yards. Once again she plucked them up and deposited them. The second man fainted, complete with swoon as soon as he realized he hadn't gotten anywhere. Winter giggled and eyed the first with a nearly childlike stare. "Wanna run again? I can keep this up all night long." She examined her fingernails for dirt.

"Who the hell ARE you, lady?"

"Aww. You poor thing. You're terrified, aren't you?" Her eyes narrowed and she grinned from ear to ear. "How does it feel to be on the other end of terror, you filthy fuck?" Winter took a step toward him and, predictably, he backed away a step. "You know, I bet you have raped LOTS of girls, haven't you?" Her head very innocently cocked to the side. "There's a rapist that stalks girls outside of this club, you know. Would you know him?"

It was his turn to stammer. "I... I'm... I'm really sorry." He backed against the wall and his hands splayed out against the surface. He was trapped and he knew it. He couldn't run away because she would catch him again. His breath was coming in ragged gasps edged with shock and sheer terror. "God, I'm sorry!" he screamed, his face flushed, his dick still hanging out of his pants.

Winter laughed. "You really should keep your dick," her left hand closed around his limp member, "in your pants," she squeezed hard, "Tiny." Her right hand gripped his throat and bared his neck. Her fangs sunk into his neck and she drank deeply as she stroked his dick. It remained flaccid in her hand. "What's the matter, baby, can't get it up for me? Poor thing. That's alright. All I wanted to do was cuddle." She sank her fangs back into his neck and drained him until he stopped struggling then dropped him like a used napkin onto the asphalt. She looked at him idly; his face had been scratched on the wall and laid open in small gashes. She snorted bemusedly and sighed. If fear is what they got off on, fear is what she would give them. She just allowed herself to remember her childhood in a foster home and slipped back into the role of the child faced with a drunk. Winter enjoyed the chance to slip back into old clothes once in awhile if it allowed her to feel anything at all. They made it easy by reeking of alcohol and week old human stink. Besides, she got off on the fear, too. It was something she could almost admire if they would strike against people who actually deserved it instead of innocent girls having a night out.

A noise drew her attention to the other rapist who was coming back into consciousness. Winter grinned, her tongue slipping between her teeth. She wrapped her hand around his shirt front and pulled him to his feet. His eyes widened and he attempted a dry scream. Winter wrapped her hand around his mouth and shushed him. "Do you still like tall girls?" He shook his head fiercely. Both of his hands closed around her wrist. "No?" Her eyes softened. "That's too bad because I want you bad, baby." She pressed him against the wall. "I want you to do something for me." She looked deeply into his eyes and bared her fangs with a hiss. "Cry for me."

His eyes rolled back in his head and he fainted again. Winter grinned and slung him over her shoulder. She could take a doggie bag back home for the boys and hopefully they would approve of her choice. She grimaced. Perhaps she would hose him down first. Winter was appalled that any human being could let their body smell so damned terrible. She giggled as people watched her carry her prize and occasionally muttered something about too much to drink when the looks got too accusing. The good thing was the apartment wasn't too far from the club.

As she neared the apartment building, she slowed her pace and dumped the body against the corner of the building, checking for lights or passersby. As she scanned the area, Gaelyn stepped from his perch by the wall, once again folding his book closed.

"Aristotle once remarked that one of the most frightening sights a man can behold is that of a great predator after it consumes its prey. Often seeming a little sluggish as their meal digests into nothingness from within. But their eyes always gave warning to let the beast be." He moved from the shadows and traced a finger along her cheek, removing a spot of blood from her earlier victim. "Fed well yet again, Winter?"

"I have fed, yes." Winter grinned and caught Gaelyn's finger between her teeth, talking around it. "You know, it's too bad that you're Guev's brother."

"I've often thought that myself;" he smirked "what makes you say that?"

Winter smiled one of her half smiles that made her look like a devil cherub. "I have conflicting interests. On one hand I like men that can handle themselves. The rough and tumble types. On the other hand, I have a fondness in my heart for the intellectual types." She smiled and laughed softly. "Too bad I couldn't have you both." Winter waggled her eyebrows with a grin and flipped her hair over her shoulder. "So. What happened to your brother, hm?"

Gaelyn's eyes went to the human she had dragged home, wondering if he were table scraps. His eyes went back to her slowly. "My brother has the ability to be smarter, but he chooses to waive that right. As far as his current location? My guess would be the interstate, racking up more miles on his odometer." A smirk slowly crept over his face. "Curious you should ask about him though."

Winter raised an eyebrow. "Oh?" She fingered her lip where Gaelyn had removed the drop of blood. "Perhaps this is why people were staring at me funny."

He smirked back and moved past her for the fire escape. "I doubt it." He hopped up and grabbed the lower rung of the fire escape, climbing it quickly. "And yes, very curious. He and I were talking about you before he left." With that, he disappeared quickly into the apartment.

"Alright, smart ass. You could have at least helped me carry him inside." Winter huffed in mock indignation and heaved the man over her shoulder again. The doors to the complex were broken and swung open both ways. Winter kicked the doors open and headed up the stairs at a quick jog, not wanting to be seen carrying a man into the apartment. Fortunately she caught no one as she flung the door open. She caught it with her foot before it slammed open, then slipped through the door. Her victim's head banged between the door and the frame as it closed.

Gaelyn was reclining on the couch, staring a hole in the ceiling. "So let me guess... By the smell of that individual, I'm going to say that he was trying to force himself on you outside the club, and then..." He sniffed the air again. "You made an example out of at least one more person, maybe two. Then brought him back here. Am I close?"

Winter sighed deeply. "Are you saying you don't want dinner? I can take him back, you know."

He sat up and shook his head. "Your gift is accepted as always with gratitude." After looking down to the ground for a moment, began to formulate ideas in his head. "Why do you ask about my lunk-head brother?"

She shrugged in a very nonchalant manner. "He's arrogant, moody, and reckless and generally gets himself into trouble. I didn't want his dinner to get cold while he's off killing himself. Again."

He nodded and smiled to her. "Well, don't worry, I won't let any go to waste. Though knowing him and his pretension for high gears, he'll probably manage to wreck that thing. He took off pretty fast when he left." He lowered his eyes, trying to hide the smirk. "I dare say he had a lot on his mind."

Winter sat beside Gaelyn on the couch and leaned back, her skirt hiking up her hip and exposing the top of her thigh high stocking. She didn't appear to notice. "He always has a lot on his mind." She looked over to the sleeping captive sprawled unceremoniously on the floor. "Do you think we should hose him off first?" Her nose wrinkled.

Gaelyn cocked his head a little towards the sleeping one. "I'll throw him in the bathtub." He chuckled. "After all, surgeon general suggests always cleaning your food before consumption." He got a rather thoughtful look in his eyes and looked away. "Winter, about a month ago, you and Guev were out at the lakeside. Something happened out there, this I know. But Guev would never tell me what."

Winter turned to Gaelyn, her eyes lowering. "I'm not sure what you mean."

He looked over to her and narrowed his eyes. "Winter, we are both soldiers, lies do not become us."

Her eyes flicked up to his defiantly. "Which night?"

He tapped his chin with his index finger. "Hmm... I believe it was a little more than a month ago. The really hot spell we had. He mentioned the pair of you were lying alone on the sand, just talking and having a great time." He looked over to her. "Then something happened. He won't tell me what."

She blinked at him, her brow furrowing. "He wouldn't tell you about that? Hm. It must have upset him more than he let on." Her voice was softer and tinged with worry.

Gaelyn laughed. "Upset him? No... Quite hardly." He stood and grabbed the body, whispering, barely audible, "He thinks he dreamt it, and won't ask if it was real or not, for fear of having the dream shattered." He took the body into the bathroom to clean it.

Winter's voice picked its normal edge and sharpened it slightly. "He isn't dead you know, just unconscious. Dead blood goes cold faster." She threw her legs over the arm of the sofa and drummed her fingertips on her knee. She wasn't about to ask Gaelyn to repeat himself. She had heard him well enough, knew it was a hint, and had always hated taking them. Gaelyn dropped the sleeping one in the tub and walked back out, leaning on the doorframe, just watching her. She could see clockwork going around in his mind. Winter stared at him with a quirky expression, saying nothing.

"Winter? Do me a favour will you?"

Her head cocked to the side, her gaze questioning

"Close your eyes and try and clear your mind of everything."

She laughed. "You know, the last time this happened to me, I nearly ended up drinking Kool-Aid with Reverend Jim."

He smirked and crossed his arms. "Go on, clear your mind. This should not be too difficult."

Her expression flat lined and snarled, her eyes flashing warning. "Good luck with your dinner and tell your brother to come find me when he's done playing with his dick." She stood and walked out, the door banging against its hinges in her wake.

Gaelyn whistled and leaned back against the doorframe once again. "Man what a temper!" He sighed and shook his head. "Control. Control, you must learn control." He turned and walked back for his snack, realizing he'd have to use softer gloves when trying to deal with Winter from now on.

~*~*~*~*~*~*~

Winter kicked the door in on her room. The wood splintered in, breaking and leaving the door without a latch. She stormed in and slammed the door even though it couldn't shut. Winter fumed silently. How dare he challenge her like that! She had thought of him, brought him dinner and had even carried it upstairs for him. "Easy to clear my mind." She huffed. "If that kid had any idea of everything rummaging around in my head right now he wouldn't be saying that." She debated between tossing the sofa out the window or sitting on it and chose the latter. Her fingertips drummed on the wood edging lightly and quickly. If she didn't think she would have pissed Guevarden off, she would have tossed Gaelyn out the window and saved herself the trouble.

It was all Saint Clair's fault anyway. If he hadn't have gone all "nomad vagabond" and run away from the manor, she wouldn't be here in the first place. Then again, it was Arriadne's fault that Winter had to be the one to go find him. Saint Clair was a whiny, sniveling bitch that needed to be slapped around. He had come to Sunlight manor only two years prior looking for his brother. Saint Clair had buried Vincent when he went into the deep sleep of Torpor shortly after their plantation home had burned down. Saint Clair had forgotten where he had buried his brother, vaguely remembering the general area of the city as the burial site. It happened that Vincent was under the foundation of the manor and, as if on cue, had woken, risen, and scared poor Ayli nearly to death. Ayli had run up the stairs from the basement screaming as though she were on fire and leapt into Saint Clair's arms. Vincent, who was very confused, ambled from the basement. He ended up in a collision with Arriadne who was coming to investigate the frantic screaming of her sister. Vincent and Saint Clair were married to Arriadne and Ayliana a year later.

Five years after their marriage and six months since Ayliana's disappearance. Only occasionally did he speak to anyone and when he did it was not in his usual conversational southern style, but in short clipped words with as few of them as possible. Saint Clair had kept himself together for about three of those months before he assumed her dead and left like a thief in the night. A week after his disappearance they had found clues to Ayli's whereabouts and Charysta, the team's enforcer, was the chief on dredging up any evidence. Arriadne had also been feeling her sister's loss and spent any time she was not dealing with duties directly relating to the manor was in bed with Vincent. With Arriadne out of commission, Vincent at her beck and call and unable to do anything other than that, Centra having abandoned the manor long ago, Charysta finding a needle in a haystack and Ayli and Saint Clair missing, the only competent member of the Sunlight Seven was sent out to retrieve.

Having picked up his trail from a sharp ear in the New York underground, Winter headed off to Columbus, Ohio and Assail's. Saint Clair had kept a special fondness for Patience after a task they had completed together. The Mistress had been more than helpful and passed Winter along with the name of a person in New Mexico. After spending nearly two weeks searching for the name she had been given, she made an alliance with a couple of Tremere and spent time helping them infiltrate the area prince's defenses and put them into power. In exchange for her service, they helped Winter track Saint Clair to her current location. He was an elusive little fuck that was for sure. She had almost had him when she first got here, too. He had been in the bar but she had lost sight of him when the bar fight had broke out. She had been forcibly thrown out of the bar and told not to come back.

The next night, Winter had walked back into the bar for a drink and that was the night she had met Guevarden. In a case of stellar brilliance on her part, she had snarled at him. "What in the hell is wrong with you? And what the hell is wrong with your eyes?"

"You know, if I were a Husky, I would be a purebred."

Winter smiled in spite of herself. At the time she had been annoyed, but he got under her skin. She had needed a distraction by that point anyway and had headed out on the deck to get away from the second bar fight that had broken out and ended up running along the beach. She had only spent about three months in the area before she got another lead and rushed out. She tracked Saint Clair through most of California before she lost all leads and returned to Sunlight manor. Arriadne had been furious that Winter had wasted so much time and had been unable to complete her task.

While she was waiting for more leads and making herself useful around the manor again, Guevarden called her cell phone. He was obviously upset and upset enough that Winter couldn't understand him. She lied and told Arriadne that she had been tipped off that Saint Clair was back out west. She found an apartment in Guevarden's building and made herself a large part of his life while pursuing Saint Clair as well. While the search still hadn't turned up Saint Clair, Guevarden was doing surprisingly better. Now he was just trying to kill himself instead of trying to commit suicide. He didn't whine obsessively, trading that in for destroying things and snarling at anything that moved. She had joked that he was turning into her, which he hadn't been too fond of. It just made her laugh.

Winter's cell phone rang, interrupting her reverie. She answered and was assaulted by Arriadne's voice.

"Where in the HELL are you? I have tried calling your phone for the last hour."

"I was out at the club picking up dinner. Where's the fire?" She could hear Arriadne tapping a pen against her mahogany desk. Winter mused that Arriadne had at least gotten out of bed and stopped fucking Vincent long enough to call her.

"Like you would know if there was. You haven't checked in with me in over a week."

"I've been rather busy, you know. Saint Clair isn't as stupid as I had once thought. I have to give him props if I don't manage to kill him once I find him. Are you sure I have to bring him back alive?"

Arriadne sighed. "Yes. Alive."

"Hm. Too bad. Well, you know I am alive. You know that I don't have Saint Clair yet, and you know that I am well fed. Anything else you want to know?"

Her only answer was a click as the phone was disconnected. Winter smiled as she closed the cell with a soft snap.

The Master of Dreams
by Michelle Belanger

Part One: Will You Follow?

Two whiskey sours had made her bold, so she walked up to the table nestled away in a shadowed corner of the club. Without asking, she sat down across from the man in dark glasses.

"You always sit here," she said. "Just watching people."

He glanced over the rims of the smoked glasses. His eyes were the color of green amber.

"I like watching people," he replied.

His voice was exactly how she had imagined it every time she pretended to have this conversation in her head. Dark and soft, like black velvet, the syllables purring under the music of the club.

"So what happens if they watch you back?" she asked, leaning an elbow on the table. His hand was on his drink. She dared herself to touch it, but she didn't have enough whiskey in her yet. Still, she managed to flirt with her eyes.

"I take it you've been watching me," he said quietly. His lips almost curved into a smile.

"Maybe," she responded, tugging at a lock of her hair. She didn't like the color. It was too orange a red. She pushed the hair away from her face so she didn't have to see it. Something so simple could make her lose her nerve.

"And what have you seen?"

Again, he slid his eyes over the rims of his smoked glasses. The pulsing lights of the club evoked strange colors from their depths. She had imagined staring into those eyes for weeks, and yet the strangeness she saw there exceeded all of her wildest dreamings.

"Maybe this isn't such a good idea," she said, getting up from the chair.

His hand closed around hers. She didn't see him move, but there it was. His long, slender fingers were like ice. She could sense a bone-crushing strength. And yet he held her gently, loosely even, making it her decision to pull away. She found herself staring fixedly at his long, pointed nails.

"You came here for something," he said. He did not raise his voice but every syllable dove straight into her mind.

"I'm -- I'm not sure what I wanted," she replied, unable now to meet his eyes.

He was suddenly standing beside her, his fingers now trailing down her wrist, almost holding her hand. He had taken his glasses off. How had she not seen that? Those pale green eyes, so clear they almost glowed, locked upon her own. She could feel the length of his leg pressing against her own.

"I think you know exactly what you want," he said.

"I think maybe I'm drunk," she replied, trying to recall when he had moved. She actually jumped when he placed one chill finger against her lips.

"No excuses," he insisted. "Remember. You came to me."

He withdrew his finger from her lips. He stepped further into her, so she could feel every line of his muscled body against her own. Then he shifted sideways to step past her, making certain that their bodies touched every inch of the way. He withdrew his hand slowly from hers, running his nails ever so lightly along the inside of her wrist. Trails of ice and fire lingered on her flesh.

"Where are you going?" she asked as he continued to stride away.

He glanced over his shoulder at her, fixing her a fourth time with those amazing eyes.

Follow me.

It wasn't spoken, but still she heard him clearly. She hesitated for just a moment, shivering from the sensation of his nails on her skin.

The club was crowded, yet he walked through the press of patrons with ease. No one seemed to notice him consciously. They simply stepped out of his way. She hurried to keep up, trying to walk in his wake before the crush of people closed back around him.

His suit must have been made of silk. It flowed around his lean, well-muscled form, reminding her of the skin of a panther. She almost lost him, once or twice, jostling through the other men and women moving through the club. And then she saw him silhouetted against the streetlights as he pushed open the door. He paused for a moment, glancing back at her, and his eyes seemed to flash pale emerald fire from behind the dark lenses.

The air outside was chill after the crowded depths of the club. She stood on the street, hugging herself, looking everywhere for him. A bouncer, walking back from the parking lot, eyed her curiously.

"You lose something, miss?" he asked in a sweet, boyish voice that seemed at odds with his hulking form.

"Did you see someone come out here?" she asked, confused. "A man – about six feet tall, short hair, dark glasses?"

"Just now?"

She nodded, still scanning the street out of the corner of her eye.

"Just you and me," he said with a shrug.

She could still feel the trails of fire where he had dragged his nails down her arm. The wind kicked up, pressing her skirt against her legs. She shivered again. The mystery man with his silken suit and haunting, emerald eyes was nowhere to be seen.

"You need someone to drive you home?" the bouncer asked, studying her closely.

"I walked," she replied.

She leaned up against the building, getting out of the wind. Rifling through her purse, she withdrew her cigarettes and lighter. That first, long drag calmed her nerves.

"Bastard," she said, trailing smoke on the wind.

Part Two: Lost in Dreams

At home, she tore off her club clothes and dropped into bed. She wiped eyeliner off with the back of her hand. A mark on her wrist caught her attention. She brought her arm under the bedside lamp. Three thin lines trailed down her pale flesh. They were comprised of countless tiny, purple dots, as if he had drawn blood from underneath her skin.

She stared at the painless bruises in the lamplight. The smell of him still clung to her – spice and vanilla and some feral kind of musk. Unable to make sense of it, she turned off the light and slid under the covers.

"I was wondering when you would come to me."

He was standing on an outcropping of rock in the middle of a wind-swept plain. Everything was gray.

"Where am I?" she asked, feeling the wind tear at her clothes. There was no cover more miles, nothing but him.

"I've been waiting for you," he said. The wind howled all around them, streaking clouds across the sky. He seemed untouched by it.

"I followed you out of the club. You left me there!" she cried.

He closed the distance between them, the expensive charcoal suit rippling as he walked.

"I was waiting for you to come here," he said.

Pale eyes, like rare green amber searched her face. He reached his long-fingered hand out to her, but she drew away, remembering the marks on her wrist.

"I'm dreaming," she insisted, hugging herself against the wind.

"Yes," he agreed.

"This makes no sense!" she objected.

"Does it have to?" he asked, walking slowly around her. "We're here. And you wanted something from me, didn't you?"

"Back at the club," she replied, petulant.

"Oh, but there are so many things we can do in this place!"

He reached his hand up, almost touching her face. His fingers never connected to her flesh, and yet she could feel him touching her. Gesturing with his hand, he somehow gripped her jaw, tilting her head back so she had to meet his eyes.

"I have watched you, watching me," he whispered, those velvet tones cutting through the howling wind. "I've seen the hunger in your eyes. And I've waited for you to come to me. I want to give you what you want."

The nearness of him, the way he thrummed against her body, both excited and frightened her. She wanted to pull away, but there was no escaping that phantom grip. She whimpered deep in her throat.

"You can surrender in dreams," he cajoled. "There are no rules, like the waking world."

For the first time, he smiled, his face almost touching hers. It was a feral smile, revealing teeth as pointed as his nails.

"Please --" she gasped, but he gestured with his other hand and she felt her wrist caught up by an invisible force. Another gesture, and her other wrist was also suspended. She felt herself lifted from the ground, her body spread open to the grasping wind.

"What shall I do with you?" he mused, stalking around her once again. He flashed his sharp smile and she trembled – with fear and desire.

"The clothing must go," he decided. "But something naughty underneath. A black leather thong. Breasts bare."

He tore the air with his hand and the wind carried her clothing away.

"Very nice," he said, admiring her as she hung suspended just inches from the ground. "What now?"

"It's just a dream," she told herself. "I'm dreaming. I'm dreaming!"

"You keep telling yourself that," he replied with a smirk. "Remember. You came to me."

Another gesture, and her legs were caught by the same invisible bonds that held her wrists. With a fluid movement of his hands, her legs were spread. She could feel herself pounding against the thong, swollen and wet. No matter what she tried, she couldn't wake up. This terrified her, and the terror only aroused her more.

"You have a lovely scent," he observed, scenting the wind like some great cat.

"Why are you doing this to me?" she whimpered, thrashing against the impossible nothing that held her firm.

"You came to me," he repeated in those quiet, velvet tones. His voice was always soft and even. It was maddening.

"You want something from me. I happen to want something from you. This is where we trade."

"Let me down!" she pleaded.

He was behind her now, and he stepped so close that she could feel his breath on her neck. His tone was deadly serious when he spoke.

"Do you really want that?" he asked. "Do you want me to let you go? I will, if that's what you really want. But," he said, and he ran one nail lightly across the skin of her neck. She shuddered down to her toes. "We both know otherwise," he breathed into her ear.

"Are you going to hurt me?" she asked in a tremulous voice.

"Yes," he responded. The word, breathed across her neck, made her nipples grow hard. She closed her eyes, unable to restrain the moan that passed her lips. She felt his tongue trace a line of heat along the inside of her jaw. "Shall we begin?"

Part Three: The Limits of Flesh

He gripped her breasts from behind, pointed nails digging into her skin. He pressed the entire line of his body against hers, and she could feel him through the tailored silk pants, long and hard. The pulse beating against her buttocks matched the pulse beating within the tight leather of the thong. He lightly kissed the side of her jaw, then sank all those pointed teeth into the flesh of her shoulder. She gasped and cried out, the cry rising to a shriek as he suddenly tore his hands from her breasts, dragging his nails through her flesh.

"Oh God," she breathed when he finally released her.

Quicker than she could follow, he was in front of her again, his forehead pressed against her own. He stared deep into her eyes and said, "Prayers won't help you here."

Gripping the hair at the base of her neck, he pulled her head roughly back, forcing her lips to meet his own. He kissed her with bruising intensity, thrusting his tongue deep in her mouth. Her breath caught in her throat, but she felt herself melt into that kiss. She wanted to wrap her legs around his waist, to draw him into her, but the forces he commanded held her fast.

"See?" he asked, taking a step back. "You can enjoy yourself. But don't you like pain with your pleasure?"

He sliced the air with his hand and a rope of force lashed her across her breasts. She could see nothing, but the impact was intense. A red welt formed almost immediately across her skin. He gestured again, and a second such blow drove the air from her lungs. The stinging thud made her eyes water. He stepped forward and cupped her sex in his hand, cradling it through the leather. The icy chill of his fingers felt wonderful against her throbbing heat.

"Not there, yet," he whispered. "Not even close."

He withdrew his hand and stepped away again.

"More," he said, gesturing. Two invisible lashes struck her breasts. "More," he said with greater intensity, and this time she could feel four distinct whips fall against her in perfect symmetry. "More!" and it felt as if eight single tails all struck her at once, in two perfect lines from breasts to belly. She cried out, tears in her eyes.

He allowed himself a smile. Then another gesture brought eight more lashes out of the ether, this time striking her all up and down her back. Each fluid gesture of his fingers brought another blow. She felt the harsh kisses on her back, her shoulders, her ass, her thighs, her breasts – everywhere at once. He stood and smiled through it all, those pale green eyes gleaming. Finally, overcome by the onslaught, she threw her head back and howled wordlessly into the wind. Her body glistened with sweat as it dangled in the air, red stripes standing out sharply against her pallid skin.

"Enough?" he asked, stepping into her. He pressed himself hard against her trapped labia, sliding ever so slightly up and down. "That was just a warm-up. Remember, you are dreaming, and I am limited only by the rules of dreams."

He cupped her face harshly and kissed her again, dragging sharp nails down her neck and breasts even as he sucked and chewed her lips. His nails continued to cut a trail of fire over her ribs and down her belly, gliding lightly over the straps of the thong. The trail stopped just at her upper thighs, where he cupped her sex with both hands, his own member still pressed against her through the thin silk of his pants.

"You want me in you," he said matter-of-factly.

She nodded, for words refused to come.

"How much of me do you want?" he asked.

She looked at him in confusion. With a smile, he flexed his fingers, and she could feel lines of force enter her. They pressed deeper, pushing her wide, churning, sliding everywhere within. And yet she could still feel him throbbing against her thong, the leather tight against her pulsing flesh. Wordless noises escaped her lips, and he dove forward, drinking them in. As his mouth clasped around hers, she felt his tongue dive deep into her, and then there was more than his tongue. Lines of fire pushed into her here as well, trailing down her throat and impossibly connecting to her nipples from within. She tried to keep track of what she felt moving where, but it was impossible. Every cavity, every nerve seemed alive with sensation. She felt filled to the point of bursting. The fire he breathed into her mouth lanced down to meet with the fire that his hands were pressing deep between her thighs. Her throat worked convulsively. There was nothing there, and yet there was everything, little extensions of him pressing everywhere against the inside of her skin.

He started working a rhythm from all of these directions at once, the thrusting of his tongue, the pressure of his fingers, the writhing lines of fire that kissed her from within. She felt herself begin to build, and that first orgasm tore through her with such intensity that stars exploded on the insides of her eyes. She wanted to scream, but she only opened her mouth further to him. This seemed to allow him to press even further into her, and another orgasm followed rapidly on the heels of the first. Sweat ran into her eyes, dripping from the damp strands of her bangs. It stung, but she simply didn't care. There was nothing but sensation.

Part Four: The Price of Ecstasy

And then it all stopped. He stepped back, tearing his lips and hands away at the same time. Her entire body convulsed, overwhelmed by this sudden onslaught of nothingness. She felt so empty that she wept.

He hushed her and she felt an invisible hand brush her hair from her eyes. She hung, naked and trembling. Then softly, gently, she began to feel little kisses of sensation everywhere at once. Regarding him through slitted eyes, she saw the subtle gestures of his fingers, the pointed nails gleaming. She closed her eyes and gave herself over to the sensation. It was like a thousand butterfly wings brushing against her. It was so light it was almost ticklish, and yet each touch carried with it a kiss of warmth and then cold, tingling up and down her limbs.

She lost herself, floating on the sensation of a thousand little kisses. And then he was behind her again. This time all she felt was a hard line of muscled flesh. The suit was gone. His skin was cool against her own, dry and smooth as marble. There was one place where he had heat, and this pressed hard against her ass. He reached around the front of her and pulled the thong away. It tore like paper in his hand. She was facing the wind and it felt like it had fingers, blowing her open, cooling her, but also making her more aware of the fire that burned within.

"Are you ready for me?" he asked, his voice soft against her ear. He pressed his face into her hair, breathing deep her scent. She nodded, once again unable to summon more than a sigh from her lips.

He cupped one breast tightly in his hand. With the other hand, he reached between her thighs, gently teasing open the slick petals of flesh. He slid one finger into the heat of her, sliding her fluids around her nether lips. From the pressure she felt against her backside, she knew that he was large, both long and wide. He pressed two fingers in, coaxing her open, painting more fluids across her already damp flesh. There was a third, and she felt as wide as she could go. He whispered something gently in her ear, but the wind stole the words, carrying away all meaning as her world narrowed down to the space between her thighs.

When he guided himself into her, the tip of him connected with a scalding sensation. He hesitated on her threshold, giving her just enough time to comprehend how much wider than three fingers the head of him was. It frightened her, but she still wanted it. And then he thrust.

She felt herself spread wide as he went in, wider and deeper than she could believe. There was a floating sensation at the pit of her belly, a sense of expansion that spread upward throughout every fiber of her being. Just when she felt she couldn't take him any more, he pressed even deeper, and it was as if her belly blossomed like a flower. Then he was pulling out of her, quickly, like a musician working a bow, only her nerves were the strings of this violin.

And then the world narrowed down to just rhythm and sensation. He slid expertly in and out of her, pressing deeper with every stroke. She tried to relax against him, but her muscles worked of their own accord, clenching to suck him in deeper. His thrusts were slow at first, working her open until she felt him bury his entire length into her trembling flesh. He held himself there for a moment, pushing hard against her walls, and then he slid out and began thrusting in earnest, working quickly up to a rhythm that pounded flesh against flesh, jostling her breasts with the impact. Each time he drove into her, a cry tore from her throat, and she heard him snarl like an animal behind her, his breath coming hard and fast.

They twined together in that fierce rhythm, the desolate wind gusting around them, drying the sweat even as it formed upon her flesh. And then she was overcome with a spinning sensation. She opened her eyes, fighting vertigo as she realized that the ground was now inches from her face. He was no longer behind her. There had been no break in his inexorable rhythm, and yet now he lay before her, thrusting up against her thighs. He twined his legs around her, thrusting further and further in. The wind blew the hair back from her face and she closed her eyes once again, completely surrendering to all the strange rules of this impossible place.

As she felt them climb higher and higher together, he met her eyes, then bent suddenly to a spot between her breasts. Snaking out his tongue, he seemed to thrust it deep into her ribcage. She screamed with pleasure and pain as he closed his hot mouth around the wound, never once slowing the rhythm pounding out between her thighs. She felt as if his tongue were inside of her, snaking into her heart, then trailing further down. This was exquisitely painful, but in a way that only increased every other sensation of pleasure. The heat of his mouth over her heart matched the heat that scalded between her thighs, and as she felt this strange, internal part of him dive down, deeper and deeper, something tore loose.

Her climax came in convulsive waves, and she tossed her head against the barrier of nothing, screaming till her throat was raw. She felt hot seed spill inside of her, but he just kept pounding, his mouth working that place between her breasts as if sucking out her very heart. Sensations lashed her from without and within until she felt impaled upon nothing but sensation – fire and pressure and pleasure and pain.

Then the rhythm stilled and she felt suspended in space. She could feel his pulse still pounding inside of her, and it perfectly matched the pulse of her own heart shaking in her chest. He lifted his face from between her breasts and kissed her with a mouth that tasted of her own blood.

"Come to me again," he whispered. "Whenever you wish."

He kissed her again, and she ran her tongue eagerly along the sharp points of teeth, licking away the lingering taste of copper and salt. She felt him draw away from her, and quite suddenly she was freezing. She could feel the wind blowing against her bare breasts. She reached up to cover herself, and her fingers gripped only the cotton of her sheet.

Blinking, she sat up in bed. Her underwear were soaked and the blankets were tossed from the bed. The sheet was tangled all around her, practically pinning her in place. She ran trembling fingers through her hair, fumbling for the light. Her window was wide open, curtains blowing in the wind. Was this why she was so cold?

She got up to close it, stumbling on legs that felt like water. As she stood in the lamplight that filtered in through the window, she happened to look down at her naked body. A dark spot stood out between her breasts, just over her heart. The skin was tender and slightly raised, and as her fingers slid over it, she felt an answering tremor between her thighs. She sat down heavily on the edge of the bed, her mind filled with the image of that sharp smile and those luminous, pale green eyes.

Vampire Orgy

by Nicholas Black

Byron stretched, tossed his third glass of bloodwine down and pondered his old friends visit briefly. Let him have his adventures, we certainly did in our day. He shook his hair from his face and tugged a thick burgundy cord. A series of bells would ring elsewhere in his warehouse loft to alert servants of his various whims, such as wine needing restocked, more canvases for his latest inspiration, or other means of indulgent distraction.

A wooden panel opened up across the room and three dark haired women clad in scanty bondage leathers, complete with thigh high laced up stilettos. Leashes trailed from their wrists behind them back to a beautiful young woman with large round breasts covered in a thin white silk robe. She seemed curious, not to mention obviously excited as were the two longhaired males pulled forward by their vampire dommes. The sleek Adonis pair was endowed with very large phalluses, starting to swell out of the folds of their robes.

"Ah! My models have arrived. And properly prepared too. Good, good," Byron exclaimed. He motioned to the trio's handlers, "Disrobe them. I must carefully examine my subjects a while before the paintings are to be started."

The vampire artist smiled as the leashed were detached and they crawled onto his super king sized bed. Soon their vitality would be his and their immortality would be forever lasting. At least in his art, if not in body. That depended on their performances.

Maybe he'd make them into angels in a gloomy cemetery as statues. So sad, Brooklyn should have stayed for the fun. Oh well, he thought, more for me, as the pile of bodies grew with his dominatixes climbed into bed behind the humans. The female sat astride his leather pants, he could feel the heat from her through the thin material. Byron licked her protruding nipples as she frantically fumbled with his belt, rubbing herself against his growing hardness. Byron laughed, fangs flashing a bit, his hands full of thick, throbbing shafts, their lengthening shafts engorged with hot blood. Teasing them with his fingertips, he peeled the foreskins back and felt the pulsing grow stronger, their length growing harder still. Expertly he worked them into frenzy, alternately stroking them in a frantic speed only to go agonizingly slow. The vampires behind each males raked claw like nails down their muscled backs, sending shivers down them.

As the Dommes donned strap ons and reached for lubricant, the female on Byron's lap lowered herself down his huge shaft slowly, biting her lip as she did, groaning low and deep. Byron licked the thin trail of blood from her chin, and trailed his lips down to one nipple, then the other. The young men cried out as the penetration from behind slid in, slow at first, and then deeper to the hilt. The lead vampire didn't miss a stroke on them while he rubbed their engorged heads onto the woman's nipples. He was rewarded with moans of pleasure as he alternated his mouth to each, licking and sucking, grazing his sharp fangs along shaft and breast. His mouth opened wider to engulf the swollen head of the man on his right, enjoying the pulsing of the purplish pink flesh. The cock on his left jerked faster, threatening to explode as the slave watched his friend while being sucked on, barely able to wait his turn in for that expert tongue. Byron worked both of them steadily, and switched sides when he felt the tremors begin in one of them, he would stop and continue on the other large mushroom shaped cockhead. He licked at the tips and using his saliva rubbed them together, enjoyed seeing them glistening in the candlelight. The nipples of his pet jutted out hard, raising and falling as her breasts heaved, excited by the sharing in front of her, her clit so sensitive to her hard grinding on Byron's enormous shaft. She slid up and down him, lips quivering with pleasure, eyes mere slits.

The three handlers all thrust into their charges from behind in unison, the vibration inside the devices humming faintly. Laughing at the sounds the humans were making, they sank their teeth into the neck of those in front of them at Byron's nod. He waited a brief moment to let the waves of orgasm hit the woman who rode up and down him before tasting her scarlet nectar. Blood ran down her breasts, adding to the sensation of the men who still thrust against her amble cleavage and each other. White fluids shoot out and mixed with the blood, the vampires gaze would cloud their memories in the morning after they healed. It would be a faint hazy memory only of hot passion. He drank deeply from her breast, scalding fluid entering and leaving him simultaneously. Taking a moment to glance up, he saw the men kissing passionately, their spurting cocks coated with cum, still rubbing against the woman's breasts. The vampiress's all three orgasm together, hard nipples pressed into the backs of their victims, the final hard thrust of the doubled dildos into the sweating slaves. The men cried out, as the vibrations inside their anal passages massaged their tight holes. The woman's intensity grew at the fullness from front and back. All three strap ones had been molded from Byron's ten-inch long member, thick as his wrist so they were stretched extremely far, the lube just allowing the friction to be pleasant in the motion. The men's swollen cock heads touched at the underside of each other and Byron couldn't resist taking them both into his mouth at once, to savor the last burst of hot fluid. His own erection still strong inside his pet throbbed in time with her second orgasm; the lips of her pussy clenched tighter, wetness oozing out. He tasted blood mixed with semen, a hot cooper and salty taste charged with energy that filled Byron until he could not hold anymore.

Byron lay back on his pile of pillows, spent as well. More servants would come and sponge them clean as they added to his glass then vanish.

Undead life was good.

Masks

by Raven Digitalis

Sol stared at himself in the mirror. He was standing naked, his skin wet and smelling of pomegranate shower scrub.

Interlinking his fingers, Sol raised his muscular arms high above his head much like a cat in the sun, stretching his back muscles and letting out a sigh. He returned to admire himself in the mirror, beginning to feel a bit narcissistic for staring at his body for an extended period of time.

Yawning quietly, Sol met his eyes in the mirror, examining their almost unearthly electric blue color. His facial features were slim and pronounced, and his shoulder-length hair lay smoothly down his neck.

Jeremy had decided to take on the name Sol around the age of 13. After his first Junior High teacher mentioned Greek mythology in passing during a lecture on mathematics, his thirst for classical knowledge grew insatiable. Luckily, the school's library carried a massive book on antiquity, with plenty of alchemical references throughout.

"Sol," though, didn't quite sum up his character. Unlike the sun, he was far from bright and shiny. His perpetual introspection and penchant for dark clothing and flowing raven hair earned him the label "Goth" that same year. It didn't help that he and his girlfriend at the time, who would later become a New Waver philanthropist type herself, would wander the local cemetery every Friday in search of ghosts for the duration of a bottle of Cabernet each.

His interests in mythology and ancient thought never ceasing, Sol had, eight years later, become quite the seasoned occultist. Though no official degrees or initiatory titles to stand on, his vast knowledge of a wide variety of occult topics and history could easily allow him to out-intellectualize most magicians his age.

Sol scratched his tummy hair softly, noticing his slightly-trimmed pubes beneath. 'Almost time to trim again,' he thought. With this ten-month-long lover in his life, he had a reason to make his nether regions look good. Andrew was his second male partner, the other being a one-night drunken fling at this friend's "parents are away" New Year's house party a month after his 19th birthday. Sol didn't have much of an interest in girls after such a fulfilling three-hour session of giggly teenage sexual exploration.

Sol moved from Eugene, Oregon with his father the following year; his dad was offered a well-paying job at a lumber mill in dinky Bonner, Montana. If it wasn't for having synchronistically met Andrew on the "gothic_occultists" Yahoo group only months prior to the move, Sol felt as though his sanity would have completely shattered as a result of culture shock. Andrew lived in a town called Helena, but an hour and a half from Sol's new location, which allowed them to meet up and enjoy each other's presence semi regularly. They had synchronized their work schedules as to be able to meet up nearly every weekend, usually in Helena because there was more to do with their time.

Neither Andrew nor Sol had much of an interest in continuing their education, but having friends in college kept the possibility in mind. Both boys were content with their current occupations; Sol at the local truck stop and Andrew working cleanup at a mental health clinic. As a result of all the people they encountered on a daily basis, both boys felt a little more normal in their eccentricity, providing a sort of psychological comfort for the deviant and subtly-destructive behavior they frequently engaged in; a type of energetic manipulation—debatably attack—that helped bond them as social outcasts.

Whether it was more the disdain directed at the frequently Republican and/or frequently insane folks they constantly dealt with, or the apathy directed at the whole of humankind itself, Sol and Andrew felt themselves something special, something different, even something invincible. Though the thought remained in the mental background when on their own, together the boys felt like gods.

"Hey." Andrew's voice came as a raspy whisper from beneath the down comforter. "What are you doing?"

"Just thinking. Drying off. Good morning."

"Morning." Andrew responded happily but sleepily. "Come here. Come snuggle."

"I'm all wet."

"Good. Come here. I've got the massivest fucking hard-on." His short bleach blonde hair was tangled from a deep sleep.

Sol laughed slightly, looking for a second at Andrew in the darkness, illuminated dimly from the light in the bathroom, then bringing his eyes to fluffy tan carpet beneath his feet.

"And what is it, like four in the afternoon? I should wake up anyway. Come here!" Andrew lowered the comforter to reveal his thin and hairless body, complete with seven-inch erection. Andrew fondled his cock for a few seconds while Sol walked slowly over, partially out of obligation but mostly out of lust. Giving him a quick peck on the lips, Sol began licking his friend's left nipple.

"Mmm, God you're awesome." Andrew was pleased, anticipating bodily release and a potential moment of Gnosis.

Sol liked to lick a spot on the body, kiss it, and move on. He did such to Andrew, inching his way down his chest and stomach, around his genitals, and finally at the tip of his penis.

"You always kiss my dick!" Andrew said amusedly.

"It's cute." Sol giggled in response.

Sol leapt over his friend, his own erection sliding across Andrew's heaving chest. Deeply buried in each other's mouths, the boys gently pleased one another's circumcised rods for ten minutes, finally bursting their semen, Andrew coming a minute after his friend. Like usual, they swallowed each other's ejaculate, bonding each other ethereally as a type of dualistic ouroboros. Sex magick was certainly a skill their relationship mutually taught.

Sol laid on his side next to Andrew with his right arm lying loosely on his chest. They breathed a bit, calming down from the excitement.

"Thanks dude." Andrew said in a monotone voice. Before Sol could respond, Andrew forcefully continued. "Fuck, it's totally late." He sprang out of bed, sprinting to the bathroom to hop in the shower. It wasn't the first time post-sex snuggles were substituted for Andrew's erratic behavior.

"Why do you always do that?" Sol said quietly, not really expecting Andrew to hear him. Andrew turned on the water at almost precisely the same time, drowning Sol's quiet words. Sol would have liked to have concluded that Andrew was ignoring him, but his rational mind corrected his emotional overcompensation. For it had been happening for months, this nagging feeling of separation. He wasn't sure if Andrew was pulling away from him or was simply just feeling comfortable enough to allow a bit less interaction to happen for the time being. Either way, it was uncomfortable.

Driving towards Bonner, the boys had spent the afternoon watching a new horror flick in the local cinema. Dressed in his finest fishnet, eyeliner, and torn black jeans, Sol was feeling a bit more awake and empowered than this morning. Andrew, who was wearing blue jeans and an Evil Dead tee-shirt, smoked his Camel filter out the car window, taking for granted the pink-stained clouds the sunset gifted the September evening with.

"Why didn't you just get your check yesterday?!" he asked Sol.

"Because they didn't have it *ready* yesterday." Though Andrew couldn't tell it, Sol's feelings of hopelessness in the relationship were starting to pique. The moon was, after all, in the sign of Virgo today. Maybe love was sorting itself. Still, Andrew was oblivious to his friend's discontent; it was a rare occurrence, and only one that happened over the phone, that Andrew inquired as to how he was doing.

Sol recalled his constant justification of Andrew's behavior as down to his zodiac. Andrew's astrological configuration was a Scorpio sun with a Sagittarius moon and

Capricorn rising. Though his spontaneous and aggressive nature was entertaining at first, now with Sol feeling as though he was somewhat removed from Andrew's equation, the personality didn't sit too well.

"Oooo-kay." Andrew responded condescendingly. "So who are we gonna get tonight? Let's find a drunk chick, they always pass out."

Anyone else hearing the words would have interpreted it as two men conspiring a rape. Though the two had no sexual interest with any of their 'victims' as of yet, their behavior was indeed violating on an energetic level.

"I don't know," Sol responded, "maybe we can just hang out at my place or something."

"And do what, watch another movie? Seriously. I'm hungry. I *need* to recharge. We do this *every* weekend."

"Well not *every* weekend." Sol's frustration was apparent. "Sometimes we don't."

"Dude!" Andrew's voice also projected frustration, though much more extroverted. "We *need* to feed. Why are you being such a douche—" Sol slammed on the breaks, bringing the speed from 60 to 30mph. He simultaneously swerved.

Sol's deep inhalation—a sigh of relief as his heart palpitated—was interrupted, "What the *fuck*?! What was that?!"

"Just a raccoon. It's fine." Sol put his foot on the pedal, bringing the speed back to normal. Andrew didn't respond. Instead, he turned the Vivisect VI up loudly. At least it was Sol's favorite Skinny Puppy.

"Thanks. Have a good one." Sol grabbed his paycheck from his coworker Sarah.

"Later." She responded, not worrying about occupational formality.

Back at the car, Sol hopped in.

"How much did you get?"

"I don't know yet. Hold on." Sol's discontent grew even stronger, having predicted Andrew's question from the moment he grabbed the paycheck.

"$359," he said after tearing the perforated edges, "I guess it's not too bad."

"That's *shite* for a fortnight!" Andrew shot back half-mockingly, using his supposedly clever fake Scottish accent.

"So… what do you want to do?" Sol asked, wishing that he was at home by himself.

"I don't know. Let's go to the bar. We can find something there." By "the bar," Andrew meant, quite literally, the only bar in the town, and by "something," he meant "energy."

"Okay. They make good Bloody Maries I guess." Considering it was almost all that he ordered, and that he went there at least twice a week, they knew by now how to make it exactly to Sol's liking.

"I just want some vodka." Andrew replied, "And some good vibrations. I'm feeling a bit weak."

"Whatever!" Sol chuckled slightly, "You're full of energy. You're always full of energy." Though he didn't want to say it, Sol had long since come to the realization that Andrew was never really 'weak' on energy; he didn't require any energy but his own to function. Instead, his prana-sucking tendencies were not borne of necessity, but of ego-based power tripping.

"It's been more than a week. Eat my fuck." Andrew said arrogantly, copying a line from The Doom Generation. "Maybe we can get another cowboy. Remember last week when we got totally wasted from psi-vamping that cowboy's energy? He shouldn't have looked at us like that. He didn't know who he was fucking with. He was kinda cute though, maybe we coulda sucked more than just his energy. Like, Brokeback Mountain style."

Andrew seemed to be movie-obsessed lately. Sol wondered if this wasn't a reflection of Andrew's mind; it was almost as if he believed he was living in a film himself.

Andrew continued, "Why are there so many cowboys in this town?! There aren't as many in Helena."

"I don't know. There are a bunch of ranches around here."

"Well that sounds like fun." Andrew seemed to mock people more than he did interact with them.

"Yep." Though increasingly irritated with Andrew's apathetic and mundane personality (never mind the fact that he feigned occult interests for glamour's sake), Sol bit his tongue, remembering his interpretation of the raccoon. Having the animal come into his sphere for but a moment— particularly in the midst of a "discussion" with his partner— must have been of some metaphysical significance. He interpreted it as a sign from the universe telling him to put up a mask when frustration is heightened, and to stay in the background, not fully expressing his anger with Andrew, or else the relationship would become jeopardized. Most of all, it confirmed Sol's intuition about not telling Andrew a particularly significant secret.

Sol surveyed the dimly-lit, smoky bar. "It's pretty dead in here. Surprise, surprise." His words were designed condescendingly, not because it was his nature to act as such, but because he wanted to get along with Andrew for the rest of the night, figuring saying anything to reaffirm their superior status couldn't hurt.

"What are you talking about? Everyone drinks in this town. Well, I guess it's only 10:00 anyway."

After purchasing their drinks, the boys sat facing each other at a booth near the back. Andrew was sure to sit where he could scan the door for any promising 'donors.' He had hoped a high-energy, youthful type would walk through the door, start a conversation with them, get drunk, and unknowingly let the boys feast on their energy. This had only happened a couple times; more often than not, the two were restricted to draining a lucky person's energy from a distance. Sometimes the effects were subtle, but they were usually noticeable to some degree. A month earlier, Andrew had decided to suck the energy of a little girl in the mall whom he deemed annoying. The girl ended up screaming and having a panic attack, saying something about ghosts; her parents blamed it on her ADHD, but the boys came to their own conclusions. Andrew was endlessly amused, but Sol was terribly disturbed, even though he didn't show it on the outside.

"I really really really want some prana. We have to look for someone. How about that lady?" Andrew slightly nodded to a blotchy-faced, drunk, grungy-looking middle aged woman who was laughing with a couple friends.

"No way, she's too contaminated. And I feel fine. I guess I really don't think I need extra energy. I just want to be with you. Just chill out."

"Okay... that's cool." Andrew looked over at the jukebox, obviously unaffected and obviously insincere. "At least they have Depeche Mode on the thing."

"The jukebox?" Andrew didn't respond. Instead, he put his right foot between Sol's feet, which were crossed underneath the table. Sol was surprised; Andrew had hardly touched him lately beyond sex or foreplay. Maybe it was his way of saying 'sorry I've been such an asshole' without actually vocalizing.

Sol responded an "Mmm... hey." of contention, fondly meeting the eyes of his friend. There was a spark of 'something' between them. Sol looked away, but noticed that Andrew kept staring, with a slight grin upon his face that could have been interpreted a number of ways.

"I'm tired," said Sol, moving his body slightly to the right.

"Tired?" responded Andrew, as if taken aback.

"Kinda weak..." Sol could hear his own deep breathing and felt his reality changing slightly. The room seemed darker. Something was different. He blinked a few times to try to get a grip on his perception. He was about to tell Andrew that he felt high, but it felt much more like being "low."

No more than 20 seconds later, a fearful paranoia flooded Sol's psyche; in a way, it seemed attached to the fear evoked from swerving the raccoon just two hours ago. Then it somehow clicked. The raccoon wasn't a message about himself, but one of Andrew. Andrew was the one wearing the mask; he was the deceiver of whom this omen subtly spoke.

Sol could feel the back of his neck aching, practically sensing the astral tentacle that Andrew bragged about using to drain peoples' prana. 'Maybe,' thought Sol, 'he knows my secret.' Instead of sucking peoples' energy, Sol would actually surround them with a protective shield. Andrew was the one doing the draining, but considering the fact that a mutual interest in psychic vampyrism, along with an unrestrained misanthropy, were the very principles that helped bring the boys together in the first place, informing his partner that he strongly disapproved of his ethics wouldn't necessarily be the most beneficial of choices. But maybe he knew.

In his haze, Sol gazed at his partner. His vision and perception were still shifting; jumping around in a blur of discomforting chaos. He made out Andrew's eyes, and though he asked "Are you alright?," the vibration of mistrust stood heavily between them. At that point, he had no doubt about the nature of his friend's intentions.

"Stop. Make it stop." Sol felt more disconnected from reality than he had on any substance. "I can't... don't."

"Don't what? What's wrong with you? Don't give in." Even in his delusional state, Sol could, as clear as day, see the ingenuity in Andrew's dementedly wide eyes. He had to make a break for it.

"I... need the... the bathroom..." Sol stuttered. 'Okay,' he thought, 'gotta go... now.' He slowly but surely arose from his spot, nearly falling over, but caught his arm against the back of the booth. With his head turned away from Andrew, his energy seemed to instantly rejuvenate. Within a matter of seconds, he gathered enough strength to stumble a few yards away to the men's room. He didn't worry about his appearance; if anyone saw him they'd just assume he was drunk.

"I'm going to the bridge! See you there!" Andrew yelled to the closing door.

After a few minutes of centering himself, breathing deeply, and actively performing energy work, Sol rose from the toilet seat. Something was wrong... something was wrong with Andrew. 'The bridge?' he thought, 'That's a deathwish.' The Bonner bridge was known for taking lives, and at this time of year the water below was sure to be shallow.

"Fuck, fuck, fuck." Despite his friend's malicious actions against him, Sol staggered and hobbled across the street; the bridge was half a mile down the road. 'He's going to kill himself. He's high on prana, what the fuck is he thinking?!' Thoughts of dread ran on repeat through his mind.

With the bridge in view, Sol's thoughts were interrupted with a maniacal scream. Andrew's voice pierced the stillness of the night, drowning out the cars in the distance. By the time Sol reached the bridge and called his lover's name, no response echoed back; only crickets graced the night.

Flames

by Mara Zoranokov

Muscle flexed, body ground against body, sweat glistened across tight, hot flesh. He brushed one hand over his face to loose the strands clinging to him as desperately as he clung to his lover. Their bodies moved in tandem against one another, connecting again and again as the lines between love and lust blurred into blazing passion. His hands cupped his lover's hips as he thrust deep inside, issuing a low moan of pleasure. Their bodies trembled, one just after the other as they came and collapsed in a mass of flesh and limbs in the center of the bed.

They lay together, both struggling for breath, their bodies tangling around one another in an intricate knot. Their mouths fumbled for one another, issuing proclamations of love between heated kisses. Sex was always this way for them: strong, passionate and utterly amazing. He had never failed to deliver and Ferdinand was glad to not be alone again tonight. There would be no more nights of his own hands roving over lonely flesh and bringing himself to orgasm alone. They were together again and the promise was always kept: they would spend the next three days in bed, fucking and cuddling and feeding each other whatever takeout they could have delivered to the house. Sometimes Maki would have surprises from the places he had visited whether it was food or a present. It was generally either used in foreplay or tossed aside to be examined during sexual downtime as they were curled around one another. It wasn't so much what was brought as long as he had some proof he had been on Maki's mind as much as he had been on his. All that really mattered to him was he was remembered and missed. It was hard being here alone, especially after his former master and how he had come to Makiros in the first place.

Maki ran his hands over Ferdinand's face, neck and shoulders, starved for the sight and feel of him. He had missed him more than he had realized. There was nothing quite like coming home and falling into his arms. While he enjoyed touring, he enjoyed coming home more.

"Did you miss me?"Ferdinand asked his usual question quietly, staring up into Maki's eyes.

He laughed gently and responded as he always did. "Like breath."

Ferdinand buried his face in Maki's shoulder and pulled the taller man's full weight down on top of him, wriggling into a more comfortable position. "And not just the sex?"

Maki bit Ferdinand's shoulder playfully. "No, not just the sex." His voice was gentle, amused and slightly irritated. Maki was always that way, quiet and introspective and deeply thoughtful and it always conveyed through his voice. It was something Ferdinand always enjoyed, someone who reminded him of someone his age in a young, mortal form. Maki wrapped his arms under Ferdinand's shoulders and under the pillow beneath his head. He shifted to the side a bit so he was resting partially on his hip and moved so Ferdinand's eyes had to meet his. "I mean that."

"I know you do," he stated, wrinkling his nose a bit, "but that doesn't mean I don't enjoy hearing it."

"Is that why you always ask me the same questions every time?"

"Of course." His tone was playful and his accent heavy as he twisted the long strands of Maki's black hair into half braids. "Would you expect anything less? Or different?"

Maki shrugged and sighed. "I might worry about you if you didn't."

"Oh? Why is that?"

Maki leaned in and rubbed his cheek against Ferdinand's lovingly. "Because we have this ritual, you and I. I go out, I'm gone for six months or more at a time and here you are, sitting idly by, waiting on me to come home. It has to be lonely as fuck for you but you still do it. And when I come home, we spend the first few days I'm home fucking like rabbits."

"We don't fuck like rabbits."

Maki quirked a brow and smiled. His dark eyes danced. "Oh, you don't think so, do you?"

"We don't fuck like rabbits, Makiros," he stated rather matter-of-factly. "We fuck like we're from a third world country."

Maki laughed out loud. "What? Where the fuck did that come from?"

Ferdinand, who was trying very hard not to giggle, was failing and shrugged his shoulders. "I have no idea. I just made something up."

"Are you going to open the present I brought you?" he asked, rolling toward the side table beside their bed. "You didn't seem very interested in it when I first came home but I think you can appreciate it now."

Ferdinand sat up against the headboard of the bed and took the wrapped package. He was sure it had been gift wrapped at the store before Maki had even left. "The wrapping is lovely." He slipped the ribbon off of the package and dropped it to the bed between them before carefully tearing the paper.

"You can just tear the paper off, Ferdinand."

He looked slightly hurt. "I know I could but I really just wanted to save it. You didn't have to have it wrapped. You could have brought me the plain box. The little things mean a lot to me, Makiros, and you know that." They always had. He had never lost a childlike sense of wonder despite his former life.

Nodding, he gestured back to the package. "Go ahead. Finish opening it. I want to know what you think."

Without tearing much of the paper, he retrieved the small white box from inside the wrapping and lifted the lid. Inside was a rather large locket. Maki pressed a button on the right side of the locket and the face opened. Inside was a small version of the snapshot Maki carried in his wallet of the two of them, nose-to-nose and forehead-to-forehead, smiling at one another. A faint song played from the locket. Ferdinand listened closely.

"Is that…" he questioned, dropping off again to listen.

"It's our song," Maki whispered, his lips brushing Ferdinand's ear. "Do you like it?"

Instead of answering, Ferdinand began singing with the music box song. After the first verse, Maki sang with him. Ferdinand wrapped his arms around Maki's neck and hugged him as tightly as he could muster. The locket swung loosely from his hand. "It's absolutely beautiful, Makiros. Thank you. I love it."

His head was bowed, his hair covering his face, but Ferdinand could see him smiling. "I was worried you would think it silly."

"Sentimental," Ferdinand corrected, "and there's nothing wrong with that. I'm rather fond of it." He fingered the locket for a moment before closing it. "Will you help me put it on?"

"You want to wear it now?"

Ferdinand nodded vigorously. Maki snorted softly and took the locket gently from his hands, unfastened the clasp, and placed it around his lover's bare neck. He fastened it and leaned in to press kisses along the chain. "I must have picked the right gift," he murmured. His lips brushed Ferdinand's flesh. "I was going to make you wait until your birthday but I wanted to be sure you liked it." He wrapped one arm around Ferdinand's waist and hugged him. "Want to know what else I have been meaning to give you and have never managed to do?"

"Hmmwhat?" Ferdinand leaned back against Maki's chest and closed his eyes, enjoying his warmth and skin on skin contact.

"You need to re-braid this lock. It's grown out a lot since you last did it." He fingered a single lock of his hair just behind his ear.

"I'll do it for you later."

"Before I leave next time, I want you to braid the other side like you did this one. I can cut it off and leave it with you so you'll have a piece of me with you."

Ferdinand chuckled and nestled against Maki's chest. "You really must have missed me. You're never this... sentimental." He wrapped Maki's arms around his waist and sighed heavily. Maki shifted and curled down into the bed and pulled Ferdinand with him, spooning around his body. With a yawn he tucked his chin against Ferdinand's neck, drifting off to sleep.

The blonde was silent until he was certain his lover was sleeping before he rolled a bit to play with his hair and touch his face. It had been four years since he'd come to Maki's home, a mere waif of a boy who had survived on rats and rainwater for the month before he'd been found. His Master had abandoned him, leaving him chained around his neck from a bolt in the wall. He'd been with his Master many years and had barely remembered his home, where he'd come from, who he was. Makiros had changed all that. From the first moment when his rescuer had dropped the sickly, curly haired boy onto his bed, he'd shown him nothing but compassion. Ferdinand had been terrified of strangers, unsure of anyone or anything but this man he had instantly bonded with. While he couldn't explain it, he knew this man was meant to be his. He wasn't really sure Makiros knew how old he was or his story, happy being lovers and friends once he'd gotten over the initial shock of being called Master and having a devoted slave. His training died hard and no matter how often Maki told him he didn't have to serve him, Ferdinand did it anyway. It was his passion in life, something he had taken to very quickly.

For years Ferdinand had served his Master, at his beck and call, chained to their bed and given meals by house servants. He had been freed only to attend court with his Master, to look beautiful and be silent and to keep his ears open for anything and everything anyone could be saying. The others would often speak around him, believing him to be nothing more than arm candy. It was that information his Master found most valuable. He noticed as he was more and more useful that the Master would give him wine on occasion that tasted strong and metallic, almost sterile. Although he thought he was crazy, Ferdinand could tell a difference. It helped his hearing, his sight, and his movements, making him much more graceful.

Why he had been left was completely unknown to Ferdinand as his master had told him how useful he was, always telling him he enjoyed his company and would keep him with him forever. It was a strange fate to be left behind and forgotten. It perplexed him, but he often thought it was because he was meant to come to Makiros and become his boy. It seemed only natural to be there waiting when he came home, to serve him until he left again. It was just as it had been while his Master was still with him.

Some day he would tell Maki his secret, but he didn't see it as important as he didn't have to take blood often and when he did it always came from safe sources. Although Ferdinand suspected Makiros knew, he would not raise the question. He was quite content with holding him while he had him and watching him while he slept.

 The Hive

By Lynx

Rain drummed against the slanted windshield causing the glaring city lights to blur into irregular streaks in the night air, the exotic black and purple air-ram car flying low beneath the main routes to avoid congestion and the eyes of authorities. Inside the droning of turbines and the rear mounted powerplant were muted to a soft, high pitched series of whines that were drowned out by music that was so strikingly harsh and rapid that only those with iron nerves could find peace within its embrace. Via drummed her gloved fingers against the top of a dual pistol grip wheel, traditional modeling reconfigured to handle the different directions that these vehicles could move in over their strictly terrestrial kin. Tonight had been a good run for her, the package made it to its destination on time with minutes to spare and she didn't pick up any heat along the way. Sure her car was faster than most, but it all came down to how a person used that power. Right now that power sat directly beneath the tips of her fingers, and she wouldn't have had it any other way. It's the sort of confidence so few manage to obtain, the nerve to break laws by the handful, to do something you know is shady to begin with and come out without any extra weight on your conscience. In this game, control came naturally for Via.

She pushed forward on the wheel and dove down another two lanes' worth of nonexistent traffic, skirting across the heavy fog that always covered the lower levels of the city. New territory had ran out a long time ago, they had been forced to build up into the heavens. It had gotten far enough that some people were so accustomed to the higher altitudes that they couldn't handle coming down to the old territory, changes in air pressure and all that. But it was no matter to them, the high blocks were for high class. Down here, this was the slums. Fog swirled around the back of the wedge-shaped car as it glided on past old neon business signs and rusted out porches that were on floors that should have been condemned decades ago.

She glanced away from the HUD readout down to the center console's LCD screen, tapping one of the navigational buttons with one eye still on the road. The interior lights cast a soft glow into the cabin area, reflecting off of the semi-glossed black durarubber skinsuit she always wore while on the job. It was lightweight and flexible, designed to confuse or outright defeat smaller hand-held scanners and could stop a typical energy bolt out of any common sidearm. Not only that, it was part of her gameface. In this line of business you had to play the part and have the right look going for you to be taken seriously. She had nothing concealed. There wasn't enough room between her skin and the suit she had specially molded to her figure's dimensions. The gloves were a part of the ensemble, the carbon fiber plated knee boots and split pistol belt slung low on her hips were separate entities yet still every bit as important.

She glanced back to the HUD in time to catch a glitch in the numeric readouts, causing her to frown and reach over to lightly tap the slanted glass panel in front of her. The display popped back to life then died completely. The turbines around her began to stutter and rapidly change pitch, the reactor behind her faltering.

"Well that isn't good..."

The alarm didn't sound for equipment failure, a sign in its own right that something is clearly not right this evening. The front of the car gracefully pitched forward and Via's world disappeared into a thick haze of murky fog, though she could feel the rate that she was descending at. Quickly she tried to power up the core, tried and failed.

"That is very much so not good."

The car broke free of the clouds, screaming past neon lights towards the ground that was mostly lost somewhere down that way. It was one of those constants in life that a person could always count on. Ground was beneath you somewhere.

"Ah hell."

She tensed in the contour-hugging seat and gripped the wheel tighter, struggling with the controls to at least try and level herself out. At this rate there wouldn't be anything left if she went in nose first, not even the internal frame could hold up to an impact like that. She tried the starter again, tried to adjust several different controls, smashed a gloved fist against the dash and swore nice and loud. Probably for the better no one caught her last words.

The turbines sputtered and fought to regain momentum against the harsh air resistance now working against them, lights within the console flickering with their last dying breath. The front inched its way closer to level and managed to slow her descent before crashing down upon ancient pavement. Parts ripped free of the undercarriage and scattered around behind her, sparks shooting out from the turbine frames and landing skids and mixing in with chips of ripped up asphalt that were much older than she ever would be in life. The car jerked and bounced with bone-jarring force as it skipped across the ground like a rough edged rock across a calm pond, something colliding with the front corner and casting her into a sidelong rotation while continuing to lose momentum. Ahead of her the road disappeared and long forgotten stairs to a subway station began, filling her with a sense of vertigo on top of motion sickness as the battered vehicle plunged down into the old terminal beneath the original roadways. A mildew saturated tile pillar shattered upon impact, the second in line managing to force the car into another direction. With a final screeching protest of steel it slipped off of the edge of the platform and collided with the tracks below, ending its progression.

She had to hand it to technological advancement, not only could it get people that much closer to living in the stars and into compact vehicles that flew around but it could keep people intact when any one of those things went wrong. With a shaking hand she undid the latch across her stomach to release the five point seat harness, about the only thing that still reliably worked after that landing. The gullwing door was fused shut, leaving her to kick out the shattered windshield with the thick heel of her boot. She pulled herself out and practically slid across what remained of the hood until she could get her own feet under her again, struggling to regain her equilibrium.

"Thought only the one oh eight models had bad cores," she muttered and spit out a few drops of blood from her mouth, colored black in the limited lighting.

Behind her was a mess. Taking out the first pillar caused enough of the platform to fall in upon itself that the stairs were no longer a viable option for getting out of the tunnels. Amazingly some of the lights worked down here yet, once the first fusion plant came online they no longer cared about the power drain from the old town's grid. Her options were limited here, either move forward or turn around and move the other way. She just started walking, her plasma bolt pistol held in both hands so the undercoil light could be of some use.

After putting some distance between herself and her

destroyed car she discovered that the extra lighting wasn't all that necessary. The old banks of fluorescents overhead weren't any better, it was the walls themselves that seemed to emit a soft glow from all around. She had to stop and get a better look at the wall closest to her, trailing smooth black fingertips along the polished steel surface.

"I didn't think these tunnels looked so damned neat..." she commented under her breath to no one but herself, feeling the intricately engraved patterns that made absolutely no sense to her.

Where had all of the old tile lined walls gone? What she found wasn't normal at all, there wasn't any purpose to have all of this down here. An open doorway led to a hall off to her left, shining the gunlight down it out of precaution more than a need for the light itself. Colored dots illuminated small patches all around the corridor, the walls and ceiling absolutely littered with ridged metal tubing and a whole galaxy of wires, some glowing and some not. Her pace slowed to a near crawl, green eyes shifting from one side to the next down to the far end of it. There wasn't a lot of space in here, but visibility was much better than before.

"The hell *is* this place..?"

The hall opened up to a much larger space that might have been a neighboring subway line at one point in time. The vaulted ceiling was the only detail to suggest as much, everything was covered in gleaming chrome detail that brought to the tunnel a deep hum that tingled the ribcage and a warmth that felt like it came from broken in electronics. Various pieces within the tunnel clicked and shifted like small insectoid legs getting a better hold on the branch. Her weapon lowered slightly as her gaze went out into the room, slowly progressing further into the technological unknown.

Another rapid series of clicks seemed to surround her, lights dimming out until only the red spectrum remained. Her vision took a moment to adjust, left with the cone of white light from beneath her weapon that seemed to vanish mere handfuls of feet in front of her. Something clanged in the distance, heavy and solid sounding. Then another, followed by lighter but more frantic sounds like something was running down the hall after her. Something with too many legs.

Dots of a deep blue light appeared in the shadows, wavering around, following the hellishly loud sounds. Something was running right for her, and it wasn't friendly. Two of them, clusters of bluelit eyes all trained on her even from a distance.

She raised her pistol at the creatures and fired, the heavy sidearm kicking back in her hands as the air in front of her weapon distorted and shimmered in a long tube of heated air. The mechanical bugs dodged around either side of it. Then they were on top of her, the first colliding into her chest and knocking her backwards with the weapon flying out of her gloved hands. Heavy weight pressed down around her and pinned her to the floor, the cold piercing right through her rubberized skin as a multi-eyed head loomed over her face. Clawed metal limbs reached out and tried to close around her, one leg ramming into the ground above her left shoulder and another in between her legs, earning a quick gasp from her.

"The fuck is this, what's going on?!" she yelled out at the creature, holding her hands up against it to keep the thing from crushing her as she kicked at the heavily textured floor, prying herself out from under it.

She almost got away before it latched onto her right ankle, not crushing the joint but rendering it completely unmovable, holding her to the floor. She screamed and kicked at the arm when the other machine came down on top of her shoulders, six legs sharing the load of keeping it upright and keeping her held down. The two of them together got her limbs out away from her body and stretched her across the floor, her struggles soon becoming little more than fighting against the restrictive suit she wore in order to breathe in enough air. Soon even her twisting around came to an end when the tip of a scythe-like leg pressed down against her sternum, a silent threat that did wonders for her cooperation.

Via didn't know how much time had passed with those two insect-like machines hovering over her before a section in the far wall opened up, the inset tubes and pipes just barely leaving an opening through their intricate weave for a heavy blast door. A smooth disc inset into the center rotated clockwise with the hum of an electric motor before the two halves split apart and permitted a figure to step through. Lighting from inside of the other room spilled out around a slender feminine body that had bulky, angular sections on her that normally wouldn't have been there. As she stepped into the tunnel the lights started to fade back to their former state, though the bugs on top of her didn't seem to notice.

There was a confident sway in the other woman's stride, her skin colored a pale powder blue in her face and exposed stomach. The rest of her was coated in a gleaming, high polish black polymer skin; a high necked jacket and full leggings that were overlaid with ridged carbon fiber plates that gave parts of her body the impression of being covered in raised scales. Long, straight black hair reached to the middle of her back, she probably stood a clear five feet eleven inches. What was the most unnerving to Via were the eyes, a vivid orange that glowed as bright as many of the colored specks inset into the walls.

A deep, almost sultry sounding voice overtoned with a distant echo flowed into life as she neared, holding a strange compact rifle in her hands leveled right at Via.

"Terragon online, level three guardian. Single target successfully intercepted. Human. Female. Five foot seven, violet hair, green eyes. Subject wearing armor but unarmed."

Via held her breath and simply gave the other woman a strange look, gathering enough nerve to ask "What the hell are you talking about?"

Terragon's eyes narrowed, without having to lift a finger the two machines pulled out harder on Via's limbs, getting a low groan out of her from the effort.

"Subject secure, request enforcer."

Via fought harder against her metal restraints, but she

couldn't possibly compete against reinforced steel that thick. The synthetic being in front of her slowly strode closer and crouched down beside her, metal claw-capped fingertips gently trailing up along Via's stretched out and armor-clad stomach.

"Off the grid," Terragon commented as she leaned in closer with a wicked, metal fang filled grin, "Welcome to the hive."

"And 'the hive' would be..? What? An overglorified nightclub?" She twisted around a little against the floor, "This isn't a great way to get regular customers."

Two of those fingertips drifted upward, around the spike at her sternum where she was able to pass over one of Via's nipples, straining out against the armor due to the cold. A slight shiver ran through her, then another gasp as cool, strong fingers took her by the neck and forced her head back.

"*It* would be the space you have just invaded, human. The space we had arranged for you to wander into. You were chosen by the Mistress for your particular skills." Sharp pressure on the side of Via's jaw made her turn her head to the side, the look mirrored by the person above her. "The Hive has sought you out."

"Oh yeah?" Via challenged, "And what skills would those be?"

Terragon let her weapon hang off of a shoulder as she reached behind her, "If you really must ask that question you are choosing to be ignorant to them."

"That's a goddamned copout."

She grinned that metallic grin again, "And you are in no position to demand anything."

From behind her back came a thick, brushed steel pair of bands that had been welded together in the center, hinged and fitted with what looked like very secure maglocks. She made a motion and the machines holding onto Via turned and flipped her over. She yelped out in protest as her arms got folded together behind her. Both forearms were covered by the shackles, lacing them together while another one gripped down into her upper arms and linked them together in back by a half inch thick steel pole. They fit too well to be coincidental, having no additional size adjustments that she could have seen.

"How the hell did you know what diameter my arms were?"

The bar linking her arms was grabbed onto, a powerful

motion pulling her up away from the floor and back to her feet. "You don't think that we would single you out and not plan ahead?" Terragon made a dismissive motion with her other hand and the two metal insects left them alone, disappearing back into the distance.

She grabbed a handful of Via's hair and yanked her head back, forcing her to look at the ceiling as she softly whispered "You're ours now, girl" into her left ear. Her head slowly turned to one side then came back, blackened lips lightly brushing against the edge of Via's ear. "Our company has arrived. Do try to be presentable."

She stepped back and used her two handed hold to turn Via around after her, dragging her to stand in front of her captor. The next one to join the party stood around five foot eight, trading carbon fiber with brightly polished metal that formed thigh height boots and three quarter length gauntlets. She shared the toned, powerfully built physique of the first, undeniably feminine, dressed in a gleaming black durarubber one piece that had a generous open neckline and further displayed her curves with a thong back. Her hair was a bright platinum, eyes a light smoke grey and skin a pale orange.

The synthetic holding Via slowly grinned at the other's

arrival. "Axis, nice of you to join."

"Axis? Terragon?" Via questioned while fighting against the one's hold, "Where the hell did they come up with these names?"

The platinum haired one had a voice that was similarly mutated into something threateningly close to digital, though at a somewhat higher octave and not quite as menacing. "Oh I like this one, she chose wisely for a change." Axis moved up close, a lot closer than Via would have liked, and likewise trailed her fingers down the front of her armored skin. This one didn't stop at the navel, teasing further along the presented body until her hand was pressed up between Via's legs, teasingly rubbing the still human woman.

Via tightened her features, teeth bared slightly as she fought to keep her knees straight. It might not have been so difficult if she only wore that material for protective purposes. Some people were too creative for that, durarubber had more applications than energy dispersement from low yield weaponry.

Axis looked over to the taller standing guardian, "It's been too long since we've had one with spirit. What do you say, valid? I think this one may actually enjoy it."

Terragon stepped in closer, her front pressing against Via's back as an armored leg came around to hook in front of one of her legs to keep her still. Axis' touch only became more firm, pushing up into the flexible material and pressing it into places it normally was not meant to be. "Best one yet. Tag her."

Via flinched and struggled to get away before another hand latched itself around her neck, Axis stepping in close as well with a thick metal collar in her other hand. The two held her steady long enough for the maglock to set behind her neck with a soft electronic beep, the colored lights shifting from green to red.

Axis released her hold and patted Via on the cheek as she stepped back a bit, "Now she won't find you in the grid. You're all ours now."

Via reared back and kicked at the center of Axis' stomach. The attack landed, she felt the light armor and skin beneath give with the force driven into her boot heel but the orange skinned woman barely flinched, stood her ground and latched onto that extended leg, holding it up away from the ground.

"And if you aren't careful you're really going to regret

being in our care. Human." Her leg got thrown back to the ground and Axis led the way back into that side tunnel, picking up the fallen sidearm along the way. Terragon boldly jerked Via forward into a steady walk between the two, left without a choice.

They led her through numerous side passages, occasionally coming across another giant metal bug doing the rounds in the supposed hive, but none of them paid the three any mind. Rather, they let them walk past without confrontation all the way into the last room they moved into, overhead lights shredding the darkness and revealing what looked like a storage room. Axis sealed the door behind them and it seemed to lock after them. She then turned around and moved to help Terragon. She gripped Via's ankles and forced her legs wide apart, slender fingers locked into place to keep her still. Via started to fight again as her ankles were secured one at a time to heavy steel shackles set into rings welded to the floor, held not with chain but a very short pole on either side that only allowed enough length to reach her ankle.

"Wait, stop! What are you doing, it doesn't have to be this way!" Via pleaded.

Axis leaned closer and almost cooed at her, "Scream

all you want. No one is coming for you."

Terragon released the locks on her arms and let the empty restraints clatter to the floor, seizing her by the wrists and stretching her arms up wide above her head. The two of them got her strung up into wrist brackets that were identically bolted into place, holding her spread eagled and upright.

"Now for the fun part," Terragon seemed to purr as she stepped aside and picked up a small control box.

The piece that her wrists were connected to began to lift upward, slowly, but she could feel the growing tension in her back and limbs almost immediately.

"Oh gods no, don't!"

The lift stopped, controls casually tossed aside as Terragon sauntered closer to her. "Can't have you slouching, can we?"

Axis was crouched down behind the strung up woman, fingers gliding across the skintight black shell that clung to Via's legs like paint. Via tried to squirm, couldn't, and simply shivered where she stood. Terragon stood before her and took her time removing the gunbelt from Via's hips, gaze hovering upon their new prey.

"You'll learn a few things about us while you're here," she started as she rolled the belt up around her hand, likewise tossing it off to the side.

Behind her Axis slid upward, hands pressed up against Via's body, passing over the junction of her thighs up along her stomach to her lower ribs. As she rose she hovered her chin over the back of Via's left shoulder and continued the discussion in a soft tone, "We were human once, too. Skin and muscle were replaced," brushing the back of her hand across the side of Via's face, "Senses enhanced," pausing to breathe in deep at the crook of her neck. She made a content sounding sigh and added "I can smell your fear. Such a wonderful thing." Fingers traced down to the hollow of her throat, "We retained some parts of what it is to be human. Organs, pulse, digestive system... They're just..." Two fingers pressed in behind Via, pushing the flexible armor into the division of her buttocks. "Improved."

Via started to shift her weight up onto her toes at the teasing from behind her but Terragon took her by the shoulders and forced her back into position, holding her there.

"Then of course there's the subdermal reinforcement. The armor plating, fitted right to your curves. Bolts driven into your body to hold everything together."

Via's head bent back and she screamed out into the room, gloved hands forming tight fists as she strained against the steel until her limbs trembled.

Axis made a calming sound behind her, slowly changing positions with the taller woman. "But all of this starts with just one thing." A strong set of arms wrapped themselves around her rubberized body from behind, circling around her waist and chest so her right breast fell into the palm of a graceful biomechanical hand. The touch got an instant reaction from the strung up woman, amplified by the hand once more cupping the region between her thighs.

"That thing would be blood."

She just started to look back to Axis when a pair of sharp teeth sunk into the side of her neck, arms gripping tighter around her as liquid warmth started to flow out from her skin. Pure terror filled her scream this time as the tallest of the three claimed Via's blood for her own, pressing her hips up against their toy's back and grinding with smooth, firm motions. The same motions that Axis' hand worked up front, one in front of her pelvis and one behind. Via, stuck right in the middle, started to sway back and forth with the help of the other two working her over, her scream dying down into a groan that was more than pain alone. Blood gently rolled down the side of her neck, beneath the metal collar and welling up over the rubber one to her suit before gliding down the slippery surface.

Terragon fed from the wound as Axis found the zipper placed in Via's suit between her legs, meant more for wearer convenience than what she had in mind. She slowly drew it partway open. She took a deep breath of the scent of Via's pheromones and growing arousal, making another sound that mixed a content sigh with a distant, pleasured moan and slowly worked a pair of her fingers inside of the other woman's body. The guardian behind her seemed to respond to the invasion and firmly pushed forward, giving Via no choice but to impale herself upon those two extended fingers. She drew in a sharp breath, chest straining out against her glossed black skin before letting it back out in a quick yelp.

Axis gradually opened up the bottom zipper as far as it would go as she worked her fingers in and out of their prisoner, adding just one more into the opening behind her. The unexpected pressure caused Via to try and lift up onto her toes again, her shocked sound more insistent than a moment ago. Black lips found the raised nub of her other nipple pushing out against the suit, forming a seal around the rubber shell and sucking hard upon her. Terragon gripped harder as Axis brought one of her legs around to trap Via's, her head rolling around to a disoriented beat as pain and pleasure mingled together into a sensation too powerful to ignore. She didn't realize at first that her hips were no longer moving because of the synthetic behind her, but the rocking motion was hers alone. She was shifting back and forth against her captor's impaling digits that continued to wriggle around in her, pushing them to new depths.

"Face it, girl," Axis gently pointed out, "You're ours now."

Like flipping a switch Via's body arched back and bucked inside of the heavy brackets, legs jerking beneath her and arms prying out against the shackles as an entirely different sort of scream filled the storage room. Her head flew backwards, mouth open wide and gloved fingers splayed outward towards the ceiling. Her knees started to give, her weight suspended by her wrists as convulsions wracked her toned body. Her arousal trickled down the inside of her rubber clad thighs, glistening against the suit's normal glow as she pulsed and writhed against three different fingers and more stimulation than she was used to handling. The two subjugators didn't stop, rather they redoubled their efforts and forced Via into a whole new high, set on draining her completely. Draining her of everything but her blood, crimson stained metal teeth drawing back from the wound to let some of it trickle out and down her body on its own. They wouldn't take her through stage one just yet. There was so much more they could do with this girl before they had to convert her.

Bloody Kisses

By Starr

We met through a mutual friend who, incidentally, had no clue about me but thought we would get along. We hung out a couple of times and then talked, mostly over the internet. I got to know a lot about her during those first few months. She felt I was easy to talk to and would tell me anything I asked. I began flirting with her and she opened up even more. I got to know about her sexual history, which was next to nothing. I was thrilled to find out she was still a virgin. I hadn't had a virgin in a very long time.

It took me a while to gain her trust enough to get her to come for a visit. She was going to stay with me for a couple of weeks. During that time I wined and dined her. I took her to the movies and bought her gifts. I got her to feel so comfortable with me that she would tell me things no one else knew and trust me with her life.

She began to tell me her fantasies. She liked being at the mercy of someone. She wanted to be kidnapped and made to feel helpless as someone took advantage of her. She could only let go with someone she trusted though. This was working out quite well.

Finally, I had her to the point where she was devoted to me. I told her I had a surprise for her. I dropped her off at the local library to hang out for a while so I could get things ready. I came back to the house and gathered up everything I needed. I was definitely going to enjoy this.

I went back to the library and picked her up. I pretended not to know her and asked her if she needed a ride. Demurely, she nodded. I could feel the excitement prickle across her skin.

We were driving around town with her trying to "remember" how to get to her imagined destination when we reached a stop light. Suddenly, I grabbed her by the back of the neck and put my other hand over her mouth.

"You will not scream. You will not say a word." I whispered into her ear with venom.

She nodded her head. Her eyes were wide with fear and anticipation.

I reached into the purse that I had with me and pulled out a plastic bag containing a rubber ball. It was just a normal rubber ball that you could find in any vending machine outside of a local department store. I had made sure it was large enough not to be swallowed though. I took the ball out of the baggie and popped it into her mouth. I then pulled out a roll of clear packing tape and tore a piece off. Placing the tape over her lips, I looked into her eyes. She was practically shaking and I was exhilarated.

I drove her to an old house and walked around the car to open the door for her. I leaned inside to whisper into her ear again.

"If you try to run you **will** die," I told her and she nodded again.

I walked her into the house holding her hand. When we got inside the door I immediately placed a blindfold over her eyes. Her tension was almost palpable. I walked her up the stairs and sat her on the bed. I left her blindfold on as I got undressed and slipped into the latex catsuit and gloves I had bought for occasions such as this. I lit all of the candles in the room giving it a warm glow. I walked back over to the bed and removed her blindfold. As her eyes adjusted to the candlelight I could see the smile that she couldn't create with her lips appear in her eyes.

I laid her back on the mattress and stretched her arms above her head. I tied each one to a bedpost and then did the same to her feet. Once I had her spread eagle on the bed I pulled the tape off of her mouth. She winced a bit. I told her to spit out the ball but not to make a sound. I reached over to the side of the bed and pulled out a rather ominous looking knife. It was commonly known as a hunter's knife and was very intimidating.

"Don't move," I told her as I ran the knife across her cheek. I played with her a while, running the knife over her exposed areas of skin. After a few minutes I used the knife to cut open the front of her shirt. She gasped only slightly and I gave her an evil look. She dropped her eyes immediately.

I reached over and grabbed one of the candles. Slowly I dripped the hot wax onto her skin. She sucked in her breath as it made little puddles on her abdomen and began to cool instantly. I took my time making little designs with the wax. When it was cool enough to peel off I used the knife as a spatula and scraped the wax off ever so slowly. She was careful not to move or make much noise but I could tell she was enjoying it.

I slid my body up hers and kissed her hard on the

mouth. I kissed, nibbled and licked down her jawline, her neck and her shoulders. I used the knife to follow my progress down her body. I then slid the blade up under her bra strap and with one quick motion released her lovely breasts from their prison.

I nibbled downwards again until I came to her erect nipples. I grinned to myself knowing that she was probably dripping wet by this time. Oh, how I loved playing cat and mouse. I took her pink little nub into my mouth and rolled my tongue around it. She groaned ever so slightly. I continued to suck and bite her as I ground my body against hers. I could feel the heat coming from between her thighs but I was determined to make her wait a bit longer.

I ran the knife all around her body as I continuously teased her. It made a beautiful little road map of red welts. Every now and then I would reach up and grab the hair at the back of her head. She would suck in her breath and smile as I did so.

Finally I worked my way down to her stomach. I used the knife once again to cut away her pants. This was a bit more difficult than her shirt so I was careful not to do any damage to her luscious body, yet.

When her pants where laying in tatters on the floor the heat coming from her was unmistakable. I knew that we were both going to enjoy this very much.

I slid the knife up and down her legs following it with kisses and nibbles. Her moans grew more and more urgent the further I went up her thighs.

I cut away her panties with an eagerness that I could barely control. When I ripped them from her body and threw them on the floor she was practically begging me to take her.

I dove into her, sucking and licking and having her grind against my face. Her juices covered me with their hot, sticky sweetness. I was gentle but urgent at the same time. I'm not sure how long I was there devouring her but I brought her close to the edge many times, never quite letting her slip over.

When I knew she was at the point where she couldn't take much more I got up and stepped away from the bed. She looked at me with a pained expression on her face. I cleaned up my face and then reached down to pick up my latest implement of torture.

I pulled the harness up my legs little by little as I watched her face. I could see her eyes slide slowly over the erection that I was buckling on. Like a cat, I crawled back onto the bed and slid my body over hers again. I didn't slide my false phallus into her at that time. I still had some teasing to do. I positioned myself so that it would slide between her moist lips and caress her clit as I moved my body over hers. I kissed her hard again and she responded back with the hunger that I knew was burning inside her.

When she was so worked up that I knew she couldn't take much more I gently slid into her. I could feel her muscles clench around the toy as I pushed and pulled it agonizingly slowly. My own hunger was building to an intolerable level.

I continued to kiss her all over as she bucked against me. I knew it wouldn't be long before her orgasm would take her to new heights. As she started to cry out "Oh God!" over and over I knew it was time. Faster and faster I drove into her, my own orgasm threatening to take over.

"I'm coming!" she screamed.

At that moment I took the knife and slid the blade across her throat. Warm blood splashed all around and I lowered my mouth to it and drank deeply as the waves of ecstasy caused my muscles to pulse in time with hers. I don't even think she knew what was happening at first as we climaxed together. By the time realization hit her it was already too late and her life was ebbing away.

When I drank my fill of her life's blood I looked into her beautiful face. Virgins taste so much nicer. I leaned down and kissed her one last time.

"Thank you, my love," I whispered.

About the Authors

Mora Zoranokov

Mora Zoranokov is a tarot reader, public speaker, writer, model and modern-day philosopher who has studied and self taught most of her knowledge about esoteric topics since 1996.

She has been published in the upcoming anthology MOTE: Magic on the Edge from Immanion Press and is working with other publishers and editors for upcoming fiction and non-fiction pieces slated for publication. Future aspirations include completing a Therian Tarot deck with anthropomorphic artist K. Lawrence and writing a book on the basics of her belief structure. She was also in a previous anthology from Dark Moon entitle Dark of the Night; An Anthology of Shadows.

For more information about Mora, her work or hiring for other events, email her at sayonarasolitia@gmail.com or visit her website at http://solitaire.empire-of-sin.com

Warlock Corvis Nocturnum

Best known for his debut book *Embracing the Darkness; Understanding Dark Subcultures*, Corvis has also released a second book entitled *A Mirror Darkly,* which is a collection of essays, released in the spring of 2006, as well as a book of his artwork entitled *Dark Visions.* Corvis Nocturnum is the co–founder of *Dark Moon Press* publishing company and editor of *The Ninth Gate Magazine.*

In his free time, he enjoys oil painting, creating works of fantasy and gothic artwork. He continues to challenge himself not just artistically but also in the literary world with new writings.

Corvis appreciates all inquiries and feedback. He may be reached at Corvis@corvisnocturnum.com or by postal mail at:

Warlock Corvis Nocturnum
c/o Dark Moon Press
P.O. Box 11496
Fort Wayne, Indiana 46858-1496

Lynx

Lynx is a regular contributor to *The Ninth Gate Magazine* subjecting readers to her often insightful music reviews.

This is her first attempt at actually being published and she is currently working on her own series of fictional books with a sci-fi apocalyptic theme.

She is a member of several alternative communities including Cybergoth, Rivethead and Therian as well as an avid fan of Industrial music.

If you would like to contact Lynx by email you can reach her at Lynx@the9thgate.com or by postal mail at:

Lynx
c/o Dark Moon Press
P.O. Box 11496
Fort Wayne, Indiana 46858-1496

Raven Digitalis

Raven Digitalis (Missoula, MT) is the author of *Goth Craft: The Magickal Side of Dark Culture* and *Shadow Magick Compendium*, both available from Llewellyn. He is a Neopagan Priest and co-founder of the "disciplined eclectic" shadow magick tradition Opus Aima Obscuræ, and is a radio and club DJ of Gothic, EBM, and industrial music. With his Priestess Estha, Raven holds community gatherings, Tarot readings, and a variety of ritual services. From their home, the two also operate the metaphysical business Twigs and Brews, specializing in magickal and medicinal bath salts, herbal blends, essential oils, and incenses. Raven holds a degree in anthropology from the University of Montana and is also an animal rights activist and black-and-white photographic artist.

www.ravendigitalis.com
www.myspace.com/oakraven

Michelle Belanger is a skilled energy worker and the founder of House Kheperu. An arresting figure of six foot one, Michelle is a dynamic speaker as well as a gifted writer. Creative and driven, she does not limit herself to magick and psychic phenomenon alone but engages in a variety of creative outlets from fiction to music to the visual arts.

She released two new books in the Fall of 2007. *Vampires in Their Own Words* is an anthology of work by nearly two dozen members of the real vampire community. Michelle provides commentary and definitions, helping the reader to navigate this fascinating subculture. *The Psychic Energy Codex*, is the long-awaited companion to Michelle's best-selling debut, *The Psychic Vampire Codex* (Weiser, 2004). This is the Everyman's Codex, and it takes energy work out of the realm of the strange and esoteric and places the ability to hone psychic perceptions into anyone's hands.

Through Wolfman Productions, Michelle appears at colleges and universities across the country, presenting on a variety of fascinating topics. To book Michelle for your college, contact Wolfman Productions at 203-426-6372, or visit www.wolfmanproductions.com

Michelle presents on a wide variety of topics and has appeared at conventions large and small across the country. Running a local Pagan Pride Day? Want Michelle to run a workshop for your household, court, or coven? For these inquiries email Michelle directly at michelle@michellebelanger.com. Please understand that Michelle has limited time and can respond to serious inquiries only.

Starr

Starr has been writing creatively since childhood. She was previously published in the Dark Moon realease *Dark of the Night; An Anthology of Shadows*.

Though she is more often known to write short stories, mostly erotica, she is currently working on a book about magickal beauty, a bit of a difference from what she has done for us previously.

Starr has also helped to edit *The Ninth Gate Magazine* as well as some of the releases from Dark Moon.

If you would like to contact Starr you can reach her by postal mail at:

Starr
c/o Dark Moon Press
P.O. Box 11496
Fort Wayne, Indiana 46858-1496

The following books are also available from

Dark Moon

P.O. Box 11496

Fort Wayne, Indiana 46858-

1496

DarkMoon@darkmoonpress.ne

www.darkmoonpress.net

The initial book of Dark Moon Press, written by Author Corvis Nocturnum, which brings you an unprecedented collection of Satanists, vampires, modern primitives, dark pagans, and gothic artists, all speaking to you in their own words. These are people who have taken something most others find frightening or destructive, and woven it into amazing acts of creativity and spiritual vision. Corvis himself is a dark artist and visionary, and so it is with the eye of a kindred spirit that he has sought these people out to share their stories with you.

$17.95 USD, 242 pages, paperback

Cover art by Corvis Nocturnum

Cover design by Monolith Graphics

A collection of essays on society, philosophy and life in general written in the thought provoking way that only Corvis Nocturnum, author of the well received *Embracing the Darkness; Understanding Dark Subcultures* can, in this volume he brings you his personal collection of essays penned from years observing his fellow man. Few authors since Nietzsche or LaVey have so vehemently railed against societal, religious and governmental hypocrisies, laughable shortcomings and failings. Sharply critical of apathetic bottom feeders to being thoughtfully introspective, Corvis forces us to look at the creature that stares back at us from the abyss.

$16.95 USD, 152 pages, paperback

Dark Visions is the first collection of artwork by Corvis Nocturnum spanning the last four years. Enter a world of breathtaking angels and seductive demoness, wicked fairies and mesmerizing vampires. With poetry, thoughts by the artist and an introduction written by artist Joseph Vargo.

$34.95 USD, 84 pages, paperback

Softly Falls the Night is a short art book featuring full-color images of the Vampire Don Henrie. Darkly elegant and wickedly seductive, the lush and dreamy images are sure to enchant. Photography by Pendragon, concept and design by Michelle Belanger.

$13.00 USD, 18 pages, paperback

Author Michelle Belanger has fascinated and informed readers about the vampire in folklore, fiction, and fact since the early 90s. Now enjoy all of Michelle's major essays on this fascinating topic, collected for the first time in one volume. Find out why author Bram Stoker wrote about vampires -- and what real-life psychic vampire inspired the figure of Dracula. Learn about the history and development of the modern community of real vampires. Explore the allure of the vampire in modern culture, and meet members of the vampire underground who have made this potent archetype a fundamental part of their lives...

$16.95 USD, 164 pages, paperback

Get your fetish fix in style. *This Trembling Flesh* features over a hundred lush and sensual images in luxurious full -color. Featuring the modeling talents of author and vocalist Michelle Belanger with numerous guests, including the vampire Don Henrie.

$34.95 USD, 138 pages, paperback

Dark, sensuous, and lyrical, the supernatural fiction of author Michelle Belanger has enchanted the readers of *Shadowdance*, *Necropolis*, and *Wicked Mystic* since 1991. Now, collected for the first time, enjoy the chilling and erotic tales of vampires, demon lovers, and ghostly visitations in *These Haunted Dreams*. A visionary artist sees too deeply into the secret life of one of his models. A businessman obsessed with time runs late for work and changes his life forever. A new homeowner discovers that his beloved residence is alive and has no intention of letting him leave. And many more... Cover art by Corvis Nocturnum.

$18.95 USD, 208 pages, paperback

The Incubus Chronicles Book One: The Jewel of Desire

Daniel Fauston is an incubus driven to the brink of starvation by the prudery of the Victorian Age -- until he finds The Place. The Place is an exclusive club that caters to the society of the forbidden. A haven for beauty and pleasure, its patrons are as diverse as their desires. At the club, Daniel is free to indulge his hunger for passion, exploring the desires of its patrons and attracting the attention of the club's owner, the regal and mysterious Amelia Brighton. The Jewel of Desire is the first installment of the ongoing "Incubus Chronicles," an erotic serial featuring the exploits of incubus Daniel Fauston. In this first book of the series, Daniel gains acceptance at The Place and finds a suitable partner to feed his inhuman hungers, by Michelle Belanger.

$12.99 USD, 136 pages, paperback

The Incubus Chronicles Book Two: The Art of Seduction

Daniel Fauston is an incubus with a taste for bondage and a need to consume the passion of others. In The Incubus Chronicles, Daniel searches for love and acceptance in 1890s New England.

In the second installment of this series by Michelle Belanger, Daniel learns that his supernatural powers of seduction are useless against artist Amelia Brighton. As the seducer becomes the seduced, Daniel takes his frustrated lust out on the young Elizabeth Boswell -- with disastrous results!

$12.99 USD, 108 pages, paperback

The following titles are also

Available from Dark Moon Press, via Emerald

Tablet Productions

PO Box 1120

Brunswick, OH 44212

What would you sacrifice for a taste of love? Author Michelle Belanger, best known for her non-fiction work on the vampire subculture, explores this question in her lush story-in-images, Fallen Angel Rhapsody. In this black and white picture-book for adults, Michelle weaves together the dream-like photography of Pendragon, the striking image of Don Henrie, and the rich mythic tradition of the Watcher angels. The result is an evocative and timeless tale of sacrifice, determination, and personal triumph.

$8.99 USD, 30 pages, paperback

Exploring the poet in his varied guises as lover, mystic, lunatic, and seer, Michelle Belanger weaves lush and haunting images that will leave the reader awash in a sea of emotion. A collection as passionate as it is eloquent; Soul Songs takes readers through stages of elation, despair, inspiration, and consuming desire. Elegant, seductive, and insightful by turns, this rare collection of Michelle's poetry is not to be missed!

$12.00 USD, 52 pages, paperback